To: Tessa

B. good

Great to see yro!

PEACE IN THE VALLEY

John T. Wayne

2-22-2020

PEACE IN THE VALLEY

John T. Wayne

Mockingbird Lane Press

Peace in the Valley

Copyright © 2019 John T. Wayne

Mockingbird Lane Press—Maynard, Arkansas

ISBN: 978-1-64570-529-1

Library of Congress Control Number: Control Number is in publication data.

0 9 8 7 6 5 4 3 2 1

www.mockingbirdlanepress.com

Cover art: Jim Clements
jimclementsart.com

Cover graphics: Jamie Johnson

This book is dedicated to my Guardian Angel. I have seen the times I should have died more than once, like the time I was ordered to the top of the derrick on the driller in the Gulf of Mexico in the middle of a hurricane, or the time I was on two wheels, two right side wheels in my convertible, but because of you I still breathe.

---John T. Wayne

A special thanks to The Cat Ranch Art guild and my friend Jeannie Edlemann for letting me stay at the Cat Ranch on Marble Hill to finish this story there.

There are two types of lotteries, the one that includes planning, hard work, and determination always turns up a winner.

----John T. Wayne

Dead Woman Crossing, Oklahoma rested in the bosom of a long wide range called Peace Valley. In the early days of the Louisiana Purchase, nothing was incorporated, yet land was available for the settling. The settlers called the fifty mile stretch Peace Valley, yet peace avoided the region like the plague. By 1867 the town that sat cradled in the arms of Peace Valley became known as Dead Woman Crossing. It was a spooky name to say the least and not many wanted to stay, but there were those who just didn't care one way or the other.

When the war ended so did the contracts with the arms manufacture's who supplied weapons to the US Military. Because the gun makers no longer had a readymade customer buying their mass produced weapons there was only one way for them to survive. They recognized the new market was west and the arms manufactures began pushing their wares in that direction. Never mind most of the men were young orphans created by the war itself who still had a great deal of growing up to do, orphans with a new name, cowboy.

The new market was west, and weapons in the hands of so many young men was responsible for making the territory into what we have come to know today as the Wild West.

The poem by Black Bart is just that, a poem written by Black Bart the Highwayman and for that reason it was left as written.

Chapter 1

The night was serene yet cold, stars winked at the earth from distant heavenly bodies. Nothing around Sandstone Lake moved, yet as often is the case, the wind was slow to ire. At times you might feel the slightest of gusts, but at others, you knew the wind sweeping down the long prairie was trying to tell you something. There always seemed to be a tragedy of late, and nothing in the lives of the people in or around Peace Valley seemed settled.

The unpleasant situation began with no warning on New Year's Eve at three in the morning while everyone in town slept. Moe Rogers was restless that evening and he'd gotten up to get a drink. He slept on a cot in his barn on the northwest end of town where he also tended horses for travelers in his stable. As he stumbled out of the barn in his skivvies he was met by a band of outlaws who had just made an unauthorized late-night bank withdrawal.

With no explanation, no thought for their getaway, every man among them unloaded their hardware into the old man's chest and the town hostler fell motionless at their feet.

The first man to arrive on the scene was Russell Fowler, the only man who heard Moe's last words just before he gave up the ghost. The speculation and supposition that came afterward determined Moe Rogers had recognized the bandits; otherwise why kill the old man? He was unarmed, wearing only his long-johns. Such truth was not in question, yet Moe died before he could cough up any names.

The old hostler had drifted in and out of these parts for years and knew everyone for five hundred miles except a total stranger or newcomer and for this, he was murdered. There was no other plausible explanation the town could produce.

Moe Rogers had been a good man, on that everyone agreed, but no one suspected the old hostler of being a retired Texas Ranger. Now the Rangers were looking into the death of one of their own and the heat in the furnace known as Dead Woman Crossing was about to become unbearable for someone.

There had been fifteen thousand dollars gold, paper money, and coins stored in the bank vault, a heavy haul, but a good one. If an outlaw could manage, he could live very well for the rest of his life. The coins and gold would have weighed a good sum and yet the bandits were able to get away with virtually every single ounce of gold, silver, and coin.

A posse was formed in the early morning hours just as the sun rose, then just like clockwork, every mile or so the posse came upon a coin dropped on the ground indicating one of the money bags had a small hole or it wasn't tied proper. For a time, unbeknownst to the bank robbers, they were dropping coins as they ran. Then two hours out the hastily assembled posse came upon a spot where the bank robbers dismounted just long enough to repair the bag with the hole. No more coins were dropped after that. It wasn't long before the entire trail dried up.

About thirty miles out the outlaws simply vanished into thin air. The posse's efforts had failed within just a few hours leading the town to their next conclusion. Whoever planned the bank job had been familiar with the Crossing and surrounding countryside. To make matters worse an old fashioned gully washer appeared from nowhere and wiped out any possibility of tracking them further.

Now the situation at Dead Woman Crossing was coming to a slow boil, the secret lives of men were about to unravel. The threat of death loomed heavy in the air like a late night fog drifting through town preparing to block the sunrise.

The town was full of wily old veterans who fought for the North or South and every one of them knew how to handle a weapon. Every man had at least one, most of them had multiple weapons always within reach just in case of an Indian attack, though the last one had been more than ten years ago.

Not much ever happened in Dead Woman Crossing for that very reason. The folks who lived in the area thought outlaws wouldn't dare try their bank. They were wrong.

Chapter 2

A lone fire reflected a distant twinkle in the immense darkness that consumed the open range. The cat studied the camp while a solitary beast known as man fed the waning fire. After stoking his fire the young man placed his coffee pot on a rock among the coals, pulled his leather coat tight around him then leaned back against his saddle and chewed on a piece of jerked beef.

A young man's dreams must exceed his fears, he thought to himself. After all, that's what he was doing here.

He was in strange surroundings, nothing like the swamps back home in Arkansas. The open sky had intimidated young Duke at first, but as he rode west with his father's money, he settled down. The calm wide open spaces unexpectedly began to soothe his soul. It seemed there was less to be afraid of out here than back home.

Oh, if only the Pearly Gates could have opened up to warn him of the trouble coming his way, yet trouble never offers a tell-tale odor in advance of its arrival, it's only after the dust settles.

Duke chewed on his meager provisions and pulled his pistol to check the loads. Then he pulled his brother's pistol from the other holster to check it. Before Christmas, he stopped at Van Buren on the banks of the Arkansas River to pick up a few supplies knowing full well the territory out west would test his resolve and skill, especially this time of year. While there he bought a new gun-belt with matching holsters, so he could carry his brother's gun properly, a new coat and other needed supplies. His brother's gun was different than the one he carried. The two revolvers, both Colt's, were evenly matched, similar in size weight, and action, just different models.

Duke had left Greene County Arkansas several months before with no real idea where he wanted to settle, but while visiting Van Buren he ran into a young man who'd already been west who told him Dead Woman Crossing in the middle of Peace Valley was the place to go.

The town name didn't seem right and Duke could not imagine living in such a place. At first, he objected, but the more the boy talked, the better things sounded. Ian Durant told him of the waterholes in the area and even showed him to the courthouse where he could file on those very waterholes.

"If it's such an easy deal, why don't you file on the water? You are the one with all of the knowledge," Duke said.

"I would love to own all those water rights but it takes money. You have money, I don't."

His argument made some sense so Duke didn't put up much fuss, and with a map drawn by Ian, Duke John Robinson was suddenly partner and landowner. All he needed was a few head of cattle and a cabin to prove up. At least that is what Ian said.

He was buying supplies back home getting ready to head west when he stumbled upon his father's saddle. He found the leather in the old general store at Gainesville, the saddle had never left Scatter Creek.

"That's my Pa's saddle," Duke accused.

"Son, that saddle was sold to me by Franklin Starr a few years ago. Been so many people walk by it I don't reckon it'll ever sell."

"That was my Pa's saddle," Duke repeated.

"Then it's yours, take it."

That had been months ago. After having his fill of jerked beef and coffee, Duke John leaned back against his father's saddle covered up best he could and went to sleep.

A lone cougar watched, sniffing the air from above waiting until he was certain the man-creature was dead to the night before he came prowling. Across Sandstone Lake an old man sat his horse and rolled a fresh cigarette. The cat studied the man who seemed interested in the boy. The strange rider wore tan dungarees tucked into small boots and sat his horse like the big man he was.

Cautiously, the cougar made his way into Duke's camp and riffled through his belongings. Often he paused to make sure the man on the horse was not sneaking up on him. Eventually, the cat found the remaining jerky and venison then stole away into the vast obscurity of the lonely night, the eyes of the man across the lake watching his every move. Once the cougar was gone, the old man on horseback shook his head, turned his horse and rode into the darkness, never lighting his cigarette.

By sunrise the following morning Duke knew he'd been robbed. Evidence was all over his camp. Cat prints were everywhere, indicating a very large predator. His saddlebags had offered up their provisions and lay open in the middle of the prairie. Nothing else was disturbed, but Duke Robinson was disturbed. He'd slept so soundly a wild animal had been able to raid his camp for food then slip away unnoticed in the middle of the night. He shuddered to think such a big cat had gotten that close without his knowledge.

His horses could have, should have warned him, but they were staked out down by the Lake, a good distance away. He swore right then wouldn't make that mistake again.

To this lonely corner of Oklahoma, Duke John Robinson had come in order to build his own ranch, his own way of life. Ian had told him something of the men on the outer edges of Peace Valley, yet Duke came to build and to conquer. He knew for certain the only way he would ever know the life he wanted was to venture out on his own and earn it, the devil with sitting around doing nothing.

Duke's destiny lay in planning, hard work, and determination, all of which remained ahead. Choosing the spot for the ranch house had been the easy part of his task, filing on the water holes, and deeding the water rights had been his first move. With that done he must now build. Ian had assured him he would be along soon.

When Duke arrived in Peace Valley he came to a place where Indian's still dressed in their war bonnets. There were Comanche, Cheyenne, Kiowa, and Arapaho to deal with, and then there was the white man, the most unpredictable of them all.

The American Indian was slowly but surely being driven from his homeland, and the whites who replaced them couldn't seem to get along with one another.

The white man had not found peace with the end of the War for Southern Independence and many wondered if peace would ever come. At best the white man had earned an uncomfortable existence defended by men with weapons made of steel, their eyes constantly alert for danger. The entire nation was still reeling from the Civil War and without exception, everyone had existed under the rule of Martial Law since the surrender at Appomattox.

Duke found Sandstone Lake high up on the west end of Peace Valley overlooking most of the country around just as Ian described it to him. Sandstone Lake rested on one of the highest points in these parts. The water encompassed a little over two hundred acres and there were a few tall pine trees about, but not on the spot Duke determined to build his new home. It would be nice to have Ian around to help make such decisions, but his partner was currently unavailable.

Land and home was something Duke inherited when his father turned up missing at the onset of the Civil War, but he knew at such a young age he could never hold his father's property. Besides, his brother and sisters were too needful for him to support. Then when the Civil War got up a full head of steam they were all separated. In order to go back and dig up his father's money at a later date, Duke burned the home to the ground so no stranger could occupy the dwelling.

In Oklahoma Territory, he had a new start and worked with an unhurried, satisfying labor. With each stone he carved and placed, the young man known as Duke John Robinson was building a ranch house, a home in the middle of long valley miles from civilization overlooking Sandstone Lake.

Dead Woman Crossing was the closest settlement and it was thirty miles to the east. No one had been here except maybe Indians of old, no one grazed cattle here and no one but a few knew of the place, provided Ian was correct with the information. He was building on an ancient cemetery, an old Indian burial ground. Many people believed if they built here they would be cursed, or killed by Indians. Ian had assured him, the Indians had moved farther west, and no one visited the place anymore, yet Duke was keenly aware of unshod horse tracks all around Sandstone Lake.

There were occasional war parties of Indians, and Duke was aware of the fact his life was at stake with so many different tribes only a few miles away, not to mention the fact land-hungry settlers were moving into the area, but still after nearly two months of building, he had not seen his first Indian.

To Duke, the question had already been answered; were his dreams worth the risk to life and limb? He had contemplated the matter for months as he slowly nursed the idea in his head to full reckoning. He knew the first few years would be filled with hard back-breaking work, but he'd always heard a dream once envisioned knows no bounds.

As he labored to build the ranch foundation he thought of his brother who died in his arms just a few short months ago. He felt pain in his heart, but there was nothing he could do but build. Not just for him, but in memory of his younger brother who had been used as a pawn in a dangerous game of life and death. His own brother, sent to kill him on the outskirts of Gainesville, Arkansas at a place called Scatter Creek.

The cornerstones Duke placed on a high ridge overlooking a lush green valley and the lake from the northwest corner. This gave him cover if he needed a fast getaway. There was a draw behind the home site which led down a switchback through rough terrain and placed him in another valley which would allow him a chance to get away under hostile fire. In the lower valley, he placed a few horses in case of an emergency.

The four cornerstones of the home he placed fifty feet apart in front while thirty feet was measured off at each end. He then began to gather the sandstones needed for the construction of his two-man castle and placed them all around the site. Eventually, he moved what he believed was enough stones to build the four main walls. At the end of two months, he had two walls mudded four feet high. He needed more supplies and he needed companionship. He also needed to secure one last piece of ground, that on which he was building their ranch headquarters, something he should have already done. Filing on the water holes had been easy. He figured getting the last deed would be too.

Chapter 3

Duke saddled his horse, prepared his pack horses and rode toward Dead Woman Crossing. He'd been living off the land long enough, a meal he didn't have to cook himself sounded good. Fifteen miles along the valley he noticed one other ranch to the north, but this was a long log home and seemed to have been there for a while. Obviously, this was the Bennett holdings along with the water he'd filed on. He pulled out his papers and looked at them to confirm his suspicion. Slipping the deed back in his saddlebag he continued on, reaching town about three in the afternoon mid-March.

Duke rode across the bridge into town with caution born of experience. He knew how things stood in Dead Woman Crossing, and he had taken the time to study his neighbors carefully before choosing his location. The town lay sprawled between two long hills encircled by a meandering creek called Devil's Bend. It was named such because there seemed to be no explanation short of Black Magic to account for how the creek meandered up and down hills until it carved a complete perfect circle.

Devil's Bend did not originally run to the lowest point around the low hills but had somehow cut right through them, hence the name. The main road coming into town crossed a wooden bridge over the bend on the south end. This bridge was the only good way in or out of town by wagon.

For now, every building that made up the town was situated inside Devil's Bend. The livery was located farthest from the bridge on the north end. When Duke rode to the livery from the bridge he had to pass everything else in town first. The rest of Dead Woman Crossing opened up from the bridge. Main Street wasn't really a street at all but a large area in the center of town that resembled a fort parade ground. Buildings were situated in a large circle about the area and the homes were nearest the creek on all sides, yet fifty yards from it. Anyone looking down on the town from the outlying hills would believe they were looking at a fort, and this was by design.

Dead Woman Crossing had been set up for defense against Indians. Every building had a way to board the windows and doors leaving only a small hole for firing a rifle or pistol. One building covered another to the point no amount of Indians could enter town without losing most of their war party. Several of the buildings were made of stone and at one time or another had received damage from just such an attack, historical evidence which did not go unnoticed by Duke.

The stage station was the most seasoned of the buildings along with the sheriff's office. Both buildings were really one, tied together by a long flat roof. A long bench resembling a church pew adorned the wall in front of the marshal's office where it had been worn to a fine polished surface. Above the bench was a bulletin board full of wanted posters. The name Black Bart arrested Duke's attention for a moment. If Black Bart was working in the area, no stage was safe, either leaving or entering town.

Wanted, Black Bart the poet! Some scribbling was etched on the poster just below the bandit's name.

> "I've labored long and hard for bread –
> For honor and for riches—
> But on my corns too long you've tread,
> You fine haired Sons-of-Bitches."

The poem was signed, Black Bart the P O 8.

Duke chuckled to himself. He had never seen a wanted poster signed by the outlaw in question, never expected to. Black Bart would no doubt be a distraction. What Mr. Robinson and his partner had to do would require a great deal of finesse. Duke nudged his mount across to the store just as the sheriff walked out onto the porch.

He was too late. The horse carried Duke over to the mercantile where he dismounted and went inside. The marshal turned on his heel and studied his bulletin board to see what the cowboy thought so funny. At once he saw the scribble by the outlaw on his own wanted poster. Scraping the poster down the lawman stomped into his office slammed the door shut and returned to his roost.

Duke Robinson paused at the front entrance looking at the pair of fancy dark green alligator skin boots sitting in the window. In an era of only two colors of boots, the dark green stood out. They were slightly used, but very nice. He'd never seen their like before. Entering, he walked around the store for a few minutes before looking the storekeeper in the eye, then laid down his list and asked, "Can I get these supplies in here?"

The man took a careful gander at the list and replied, "Everything but the salt pork. You'll have to get that from Claude Pepper across the way."

"Thank you. I'll be back in about an hour to pick up my order."

"I'll have it ready for you, young man. What's the name you want on it?"

"Duke Robinson."

"There's no credit here until I get to know you. You won't be needin' any credit I hope," the store owner said.

"I won't be needin' any credit," Duke responded while studying the man with wary eyes. The store owner perfectly fit the description he'd been given.

"Now, a young man like you what don't need credit, don't that beat all."

"I've done all right so far, Mr. Lane. And I'll continue to do just fine as long as everyone minds their own business." Turning on the ball of his foot he headed out the door pulling it shut behind him.

Scranton Lane studied the young man with wide eyes as he left the building, rubbing his whiskered jaw steeped in contemplation. Seemed to him like the young man was setting up shop somewhere near Peace Valley and there was no denying the fact the country needed new blood, as long as it was good blood.

Studying the list once again Scranton decided the young man would bear watching, not to make sure he fared well, but to see how far he went. The list he'd handed Scranton was dead on what a man would need if he was going to winter out on the prairie somewhere. To top that off, the only land in the area that hadn't been settled on was owned by him. Naturally, the store owner began to wonder, just where did the boy intend settling? Every water hole in the territory was claimed by someone, and that left little to nothing for any newcomers. The old man scratched his head as he studied the list looking for some sort of clue. Surely there would be something on which he could build an idea.

There, right at the bottom of the list, he found what he was looking for. Four hundred rounds of ammo! Scranton Lane swallowed hard. He did not like the idea forming in his head, but he considered no other.

Chapter 4

The Divine Watering Hole was a corner saloon where a man with money could get a drink and pick up information. Duke pushed open the bat-winged doors and stepped inside letting his eyes adjust to the darkness before taking a look around. Slipping his hat from his head he hung it on the hat rack near the door and made his way to a table along the back wall. He sat facing the door where he placed his rifle against the wall. With the ease of long practice, he slipped his six-shooter from its holster and laid it across the table in front of him. Every head in the place turned in his direction at the sound of the pistol hitting the table top, but that was only three men including the bartender.

The last thing Duke wanted right now was trouble, but trouble usually determined what a man did and this day was no different. There were two men in the place having a drink, one was a tall lanky fellow still wearing his hat and the other was a few inches shorter and wider at the shoulders and hip. Both men wore tied down guns. Otherwise only the bartender was there to witness.

"What would you like young man," the bartender asked.

Duke measured the man long and slow. "How about a shot of whisky and a cold beer if you have one."

"The whisky ain't no trouble, but all I have is room temperature beer."

"That'll do." At seventeen, Duke had known plenty of trouble. He had lost both parents by the age of fifteen while the Civil War was raging back east. He hailed from the flats outside of Pocahontas Arkansas, a place called the De'Laplaine swamp. He knew how to take care of himself.

He eyed the two men across the room and knew them for the trouble they were. With any luck, he could have his beer, pay the bartender and get out of town before they pushed matters.

He'd seen their kind before. Of course, often times when a man young or old entered a saloon someone was apt to say something; hello, how are you, or you sure look worn out, look what the cat dragged in, any number of cordial greetings, any one of them would have been preferred to the one he actually got.

"Son, if you were any younger you'd still be in diapers," the short stocky fellow teased.

The bartender slowly sat Duke's drinks on the table, hesitantly scraped up the two bits and ducked back behind the bar. Duke downed the shot of whisky and looked as though he was going to pick up his beer when he lifted his revolver from the table and pointed it at the two men before they knew he had it in his hand.

"I can abide some amount of funning from friends of mine, but from a complete and total stranger, I haven't the patience. Now you will apologize," Duke waved his gun.

"Like hell I..."

A bullet lifted Slim's hat from his head. He jerked back, taking both him and the chair to the floor. Holding his hands high for all to witness, he remained deathly still.

"You get one more chance and then I'm going to walk out of here soon as I finish my beer, but you never will if you don't apologize right now."

The man looked down at his friend on his back. He realized with a coward's disposition he was not the man he thought he was. He knew the young man, at least ten years younger, had just bested him and his partner, making them appear the fool. The thought rankled, but he also knew guns didn't care who pulled the trigger. The corresponding result would still be the same.

"I'm sorry," he started to say "boy" but thought better of it. "My tongue gets the better of me sometimes."

Duke lowered the cocked hammer and picked up his beer with his left hand. He took a good swallow, but his gun never wavered, hovering ominously a few inches above the table. Still, no one moved, for the young stranger had not replied. Everyone expected a response, yet none was offered. He lifted his mug and took another sip of warm beer.

Just then the town marshal pushed open the batwing doors and stepped inside. "What's going on in here," he demanded.

Duke answered for them. "We're just getting to know one another. You can join us if you like."

The marshal studied Duke for a moment and then turned his attention to the two men at the other table. "I've told you two you were going to get yourselves killed if you're not careful. Your big mouth almost got it done today. Get up Marty, pick up your hat and right your chair."

Marty did as he was told and took his seat, never allowing any unwarranted motion, never looking in the direction of the young man whose gun was still trained on them. Marty was well aware of his disadvantage now the town law was present.

"My name is Marshal Fowler. You can put your weapon away, young man. I'll be right here until you leave town."

Duke laid his pistol on the table where it was within easy grasp yet still pointing at the men across the room. He sipped his beer and stared.

Marshal Russell Fowler walked up to the bar. "Set me up, Harvey."

After a few quiet minutes alone with his beer, Duke picked up his guns and walked out the door. He paused on the boardwalk. On a distant hill, he could see an old man sitting his horse. An odd place for anyone to be, but there he was looking over the entire town sizing things up like a general getting ready to do battle.

Duke walked down the street and picked up his salt pork from Claude Pepper and when Duke entered the store across the street he walked to the counter and took a seat on the stool at the end of the wall. His supplies seemed to be in order, but first things first. "You own the rights to Sandstone Lake," Duke said.

"Now how could you possibly know such a thing?"

"I ran into a fellow a few months back in Arkansas. His name was Ian Durant, he's my partner. Said, if I was planning to settle in these parts I should look you up."

"He did, did he?"

"My father once told me, Duke, as long as a man has the right documents or papers backing his play he'll do just fine, but a man who doesn't get things lined up legal will soon find himself playing the game of life with a cold deck of cards. I figure he's right."

"That's nice, but what does any of that have to do with me?" the store keeper asked with a cautious eye.

"I..." Duke paused, "...we want to buy it." The young man could have dropped a sledge hammer easier, but he confirmed Mr. Lane's suspicion.

"Who is we?"

"Me and my partner, Ian Durant."

"You partners with that sidewinder?"

"I'm not sure I follow you."

"He left here owing me near fifty dollars. Said he'd have it for me in short order, instead he cut and run."

Duke had to think fast. He had not expected this. "Did you ever stop to think he was coming back once he had the money?"

"No I never stopped to think anything, only he still owes me forty seven dollars and seven cents."

Duke pulled out his wallet and counted out fifty dollars, then handed it to the man. I don't want our ranch to start off on the wrong foot. Here's your money. Now, how about the place?"

"Son, in the first place anyone who goes over into that country and tries to settle on that lake will be shot post haste. In the second, I don't want to sell. I like my land. And third, it wouldn't do you one bit of good. Not unless you can get old man Bennett and his boys to let you cross their land, which they won't. They own everything on all sides of my property. The only reason I don't get shot when I go wondering off up there is because they have to buy their goods somewhere. Were they to shoot me they'd have to ride three hundred miles once a month just to keep their ranch going."

"Our ranch," Duke corrected.

"Our ranch?" Scranton Lane shifted uneasy.

"Ian Durant and I filed on that land more than two months ago. I'm building our home ranch up on Sandstone Lake as we speak."

"You what?" Scranton Lane almost swallowed his unlit cigar.

"I figured with your water rights and the ones we already own I'll have most all of the country west of here sewn up."

"The only thing you are going to own is a grave on boot hill son. The Bennett's have six boys and three girls, all of which can shoot a running deer from five hundred yards. They eat well and fight like a well-trained army. He also employee's about twenty-five hard scrabble riders most of the time and they double as warriors. All you've done is given them a good reason to shoot you."

"Will you sell Sandstone Lake to us or not?" Duke was growing impatient.

"Depends. The bank was robbed a few months back, a year ago to be exact. You're mighty young to be so free with the kind of money you're spreading around. How'd you come by it?"

"My old man used to bury his money around our house in mason jars. I watched him. When he died I knew right where his money was hid. Ma, she died a few years earlier so I burned the cabin and went to St. Louis. When I was big enough I went home dug up all that money and headed west. I saw that high up valley of yours and I knew I had found my new home, providing you'll sell it to me."

"Why did you burn the cabin?" Lane asked. "That part don't make no sense."

"If someone moved in and took over while I was away, I'd never be able to dig up the jars of money when I came home, not without a fight."

Scranton Lane measured the young man through a long silence. "You the one who fired that shot I heard a little while ago?"

"Yes sir, I was defending my honor. I won't stand being picked on by strangers," Duke said.

"Oh hell, it's no skin off'n my back if you get yourself kilt." Turning abruptly the storekeeper dropped to his safe and dialed the combination. A moment later he produced the papers that held the land rights Duke wanted. "I figure the place is worth an even five hundred," Lane said.

"What if I give you two hundred now and the rest in the spring?"

"You mean if you're alive, don't you? No, I'd better receive payment in full or I'll just put the deed right back in my safe."

"All right, but I might need credit before this fall if I do things your way."

"I can arrange credit for you, but I can't carry you for a long time. I need balances paid every three months," Scranton said.

"That would work just fine. I'll have more money out here by then."

"What are you planning to do? Rob the bank?"

"No sir, I'll be bringing in beef. I've already registered my brand with the Stockman's Association."

"And what brand would that be?"

"The circle R."

Scranton Lane didn't overlook the fact a circle B could be placed right over the circle R and no one would know the difference, but then the Bennett's wouldn't be stealing their own beef. Taking another look at the young man before him he didn't figure Duke Robinson for a thief either. Lane signed the deed and pushed it over to Duke. Then he took up the five hundred dollars the boy laid on the counter. He counted through it once and placed the money in his safe. He counted the money with two purposes in mind. One to make sure it was all there and two he wanted to make sure none of the greenbacks were augmented with Confederate notes a few people had tried on him of late. The Confederate notes looked real enough, but they were worthless now that the war was over.

"I'll put the balance of the fifty on your account to the good."

"That will be just fine."

Duke paid for his other goods and packed the items on his horses. Last of all, he picked up the ammunition he'd ordered, scraping it into a burlap bag capable of carrying the four hundred rounds of .44's.

"You stocking up for a war I don't know about?"

"I just like to be certain I'm well armed. There are Indian's over that way, leastways I keep seeing sign and I don't want to get caught short handed. Have you ever tried to stave off an Indian attack with one pistol, one rifle and twenty two rounds of ammunition?"

"Can't say as I have."

"I don't ever want to be in that situation again. You have got to kill an Indian every time you pull the trigger and hope they give up before you get to your last bullet."

"I take it you've been there," Scranton said.

23

"I got lucky the first time. I don't ever want to have to count on that much luck all by itself ever again if you get my meaning."

Scranton Lane watched as Duke placed the ammunition in his saddlebags, secured his supplies on his pack horses and mounted up. The young ranch owner waved his hand at the store keeper and then turned his horses up the street. Scranton smiled to himself. This was going to be more fun to watch than a fist fight at the Saturday night dance. If he was lucky, when the dust settled he'd still own the lake and be five hundred dollars richer. Of course that all depended on how much the boy knew about legality.

Chapter 5

Duke lumbered along at an easy canter three miles southwest of town with his pack horses in tow. Dust was kicked up by the wind here and there from a storm on the horizon. It was a cold bone-chilling wind, but it wasn't quite cold enough to snow. He grumbled something about his luck and pulled a slicker from the back of his horse. Cottonwood trees leaned with the wind bending them as the approaching storm gathered steam. The larger trees stood straight then leaned to the point of almost breaking. The only thing not blowing in the wind seemed to be solid rock and Duke knew he would be next if he didn't find cover from the approaching storm.

The young cowboy dipped his head low to keep the blowing sand and other debris out of his eyes, chancing a look only when the wind lifted momentarily so as not to lose his valued hat. A cowboy hat will stick to your head like glue if you know how to wear one, never offering up the need to go chasing your hat because the wind was too strong. This technique is the one Duke used now. The harder the wind blew, the tighter his hat gripped his skull.

For better or worse his plans were underway. He'd gone to town and made the deal needed for the new ranch. In a few short days, he would be a target for every gun hand in Oklahoma. Now all he had to do was wait. He owned all water rights for one hundred fifty miles, he was proving up on the home ranch already and from there he could command the entire countryside for hundreds of square miles. The fact that other ranches dotted the landscape was not a consideration; those squatters would have to move. Ian and Duke now owned all their water rights.

With the purchase of Sandstone Lake and the land surrounding it he was short on cash, but he had all the necessary supplies. There were cattle back in the breaks west of his place which he could brand and push out onto the range. He could brand a good many of them before anyone spotted his first circle R Spring roundup would come, but that was weeks away.

The sky grew dark. Lightning flashed and he glimpsed a shelter. It wasn't much but did offer a respite from the wind and the coming storm. The clouds were gathering darker on the western horizon as he shuffled for cover. West was the direction he had to ride in order to reach home. Making for a low hanging cliff just to the north he reined in and unsaddled his horse, throwing everything to the back of the shelter as quickly as possible. Then he removed the burden on his pack horses. He had a few minutes to gather sticks and larger wood for a quick fire and then the cold wind-driven rain was on him. His horses crowded in under the overhang not wanting to be in the downpour.

Keeping it away from his supplies, Duke built a fire in the far back corner away from the wind knowing he would be spending the night. He didn't want to camp here, but a ride home in such weather was not to his liking.

Once the fire was going good he dug out his cup and a little coffee. Having left his coffee pot at the home site he sprinkled a bit of grounds into the bottom of his new cup then held it out to catch water running off the rocks above. In a few moments, he had a cup full of water. Then he sat the cup on his strategically placed rock in the fire to bring it to a boil. Once the coffee boiled he took it off with gloved hands and let the java cool to a point he could drink.

At the right moment, Duke picked up his coffee and took a sip. It was good, the grounds had settled to the bottom and he could drink most all of it before he encountered them. He leaned back against his saddle and looked out into the dark rainy night. Lightning flashed and he saw a rider sitting his horse out by the road a hundred yards off, a big man, the same man he'd seen earlier sizing up the town. When the lightning flashed again a few seconds later the rider was gone. Duke was so startled he jumped to his feet, rushing to the edge of the overhang.

Who in their right mind would be out in a storm like this? Had he known of the place, but Duke had beat him to it? Or was the man following him? If so, why? He stared out into the driving rain, searching during lightning flashes for any sign of the the man. Nothing. Duke shook his head and returned to the fire. No one but the store keeper knew of his plans, or the water rights. Why would anyone be following him this quickly? He expected trouble down the line, but not tonight. He shucked his pistol and checked the loads, wiping it down; ready for anything that might happen. He'd have to watch himself from now on.

Odd for a man to ride so close to town but turn away at the last minute on a stormy night such as this, but who was to say for what reason a man would do such a thing. Duke could think of no reason not to ride for the shelter of town. In fact, had he been paying attention instead of engrossed in what he was about to do, he would have checked into the hotel and would now be resting comfortably in his own dry bed.

The tempest continued throughout the night and dawn arrived with no relief in sight. Duke tossed more sticks on the fire and leaned back to watch the raging storm. It was a cold rain on the verge of snow. His horses were doing fine as horses go. Mid-morning saw the first sign of a let up in hostilities from Mother Nature and Duke saddled his dun. Packing his recent purchases tightly he mounted up and led his pack horses back to the main road.

A glimpse of red caught his attention. Red like that was out of place in the dirt and he rode closer. The body of a man was sprawled in a grotesque position, gun in hand. He had not heard any gunfire during the night, but with all the lightning and thunder, Duke figured he would not have heard even if he'd been wide awake. As he dismounted and leaned over the corpse he realized it was slim, one of the men he'd braced in the saloon the day before. "Marty, that's your name."

Duke checked the man's pockets and removed what he could find. Then he unbuckled the man's gun belt and tossed it over his saddle horn. So, someone had not taken a liking to the man after all. He looked around for tracks from the night before, but it had rained so hard there was nothing but the tracks he was now making. Then he realized this was the spot where he'd seen the rider the night before. Who was the old man? What was he after? Looking around Duke wondered how the man had disappeared so quickly and without a trace. There were no hills to hide behind, no steep slopes, no trees, nothing. The lightning strikes at the time had been so close, his disappearance made no sense. Lightning had lit up the sky for several minutes almost nonstop, yet the rider had vanished in the blink of an eye.

Stepping back into leather he headed for town and the marshal's office. No one was in, but the restaurant down the street was open so he ambled down to the establishment and stepped down. Wrapping his reins and lead ropes around the hitching post he stepped up on the boardwalk and pushed the door open. Looking around he saw the marshal and walked over to his table.

"I thought you ought to know, there's a dead man on the road outside of town."

"Who is he?"

"That fellow from the saloon yesterday, the one you called Marty."

Jumping up the marshal grabbed his hat and headed out the door on the run. He ran for the stables where a few minutes later he emerged on a sorrel horse and galloped out of town. Duke watched from the door of the café as the marshal turned west once he crossed the bridge. Figuring the marshal could handle things Duke sat down at a nearby table and ordered breakfast. Might as well get a good meal, he figured, knowing the lawman would be back to talk to him.

"What's for you stranger," the young lady asking was of a nice build and had a rather pretty smile accented by high cheekbones. She wore a red and blue colored dress which gave off a hint of purple if you looked at the design just right. She wore an apron about her waist and began pouring coffee from the pot she carried into the room.

"What have you got?" Duke was unsure what the western fare might be. The last time he'd eaten any kind of real breakfast was when he left home and traipsed down into south Arkansas. There he was able to get grits eggs and bacon, yet Arkansas was an entirely different part of the country.

"I can fix up some eggs and if you are real hungry we have some leftover chili from last night," the young lady said.

"I'll take three eggs and slop some of that chili on top of them. I'm hungry. Some biscuits if you've got them," he added.

"We call them corn dodgers out here." The girl spun on her toes and went back to the kitchen. A few minutes later she returned with the eggs smothered in chili and two fresh corn dodgers. "If you need anything else, just shout."

Duke ate like a hog to slop and before the waitress could return to refill his coffee he was finished. Growing up on the streets or in an orphanage doesn't bode well for manners when a young man is hungry. Today offered no immunity.

"My, you polished that off in a hurry. Do you want something more?"

"No ma'am, just coffee."

The young lady topped off his coffee and took his empty plate. He watched as she sashayed her way back to the kitchen. She was pretty. In fact, she was almost too pretty. Duke felt a strange feeling as if this was the girl for him, only he couldn't say why.

Then Duke leaned back and closed his eyes for a moment. He was trying to remember the faces of his mother and father, but they wouldn't come to him. Too much time had passed for him to remember. He had no picture, the only one he'd found was lost in the Mississippi River when he crossed over to Reelfoot Lake with Captain Grimes several years before, and that during the Civil War.

Chapter 6

Presently a buckboard rattled out of town with two men and Duke waited. No doubt the marshal would want to talk to him. Though he could offer no enlightenment, he knew enough to wait. The morning labored on and he'd almost drank his fill of coffee when he saw the buckboard returning with the marshal riding shotgun. At the café, the driver drew to a stop in the muddy street. Duke almost choked on his last of his coffee. There were two bodies in the wagon and the second was Marty's friend. The two men Duke had trouble with the day before were both dead!

There were two horses tied behind the wagon and the marshal's horse made three. Where had the other body been? Why hadn't he seen it when he found the first man? Slowly Duke got up and went to the front door and stepped out onto the boardwalk, looked down at the wagon, then up at the marshal.

"I found some papers on the slim man," he said. "I didn't know there were two bodies."

"Let me see what you found," the marshal said.

He went to his horse, opened the flap on his saddlebag and pulled out everything he had taken off Marty and handed the items to the marshal. The lawman hopped down from the wagon onto the boardwalk. Taking the evidence he rifled through the papers quickly and then laid them on the wagon next to the driver. Suddenly he unlimbered his pistol and pointed it at Duke standing less than three feet away.

"I'm going to have to hold you on suspicion of murder," the marshal said.

"What?"

"You heard me, now unbuckle your gun belt, slowly." The pistol waved again.

"But, I haven't done anything," Duke protested.

"Didn't you have a run in with these fellows yesterday over at the saloon?"

"You know I did, you were there, but I forgot all about them the moment I walked out."

"They didn't. Most of the town overheard them last night. They went gunning for you, said they were going to put the little whelp in his place."

Duke swallowed the realization hard, then slowly reached for the buckle on the gun belt he was wearing and unbuckled his weapons. He relinquished his guns to the lawman. So this was how a dream ended!

"If I had gunned them down, which I didn't, wouldn't I have the right to defend myself?"

"Most certainly, but in this instance, both men were murdered," the marshal explained.

"How do you know it was murder?"

"When a man is gunned down head on, there is room for doubt, when he's shot in the back, we call it murder."

The marshal waved his gun indicating Duke should walk in front of him to the jail. Slowly he paced off the steps that would confine him. Murder! How could he have been so easily framed for such a crime? Someone must know what he was up to, but Scranton Lane was the only person in town who knew anything of his plans unless he had blabbed. What about the stranger on the horse, the one he saw in the middle of the storm? The man had been sitting his horse right where he found Marty's body.

As the men made their way down the long boardwalk, Duke paused at Scranton Lane's store and looked in the window at the green alligator boots on display. Marshal Fowler pushed his revolver into Duke's back.

"Move on son, you sure ain't going to need those boots, not now you ain't."

Duke paused at the doorway to the marshal's office and felt the cold steel of the marshal's revolver in the center of his back once again. Without turning, he headed to the back of the jail where he had a choice of three cells.

The cell door clanged shut behind him. Duke was growing worried. His saddlebags contained everything indicating his plans, what he had done and what he was planning to do. Even if Scranton Lane had said nothing, soon the whole territory would know he had filed on all of the water in Peace Valley to include the Bennett holdings, the McCarver spread to the south, the abandoned Sagebrush Mine and the Ferguson place.

One of the men from the buckboard stepped into the marshal's office.

"Wally," the marshal said, "go find Jack. He was in town last night, so he should be around."

Duke leaned against the bars. "Marshal, I have deeds to land and claims in my saddlebags. I would appreciate it if you would get them and bring them to me. I would consider it a favor."

"I'll go get your saddlebags, but they are remanded to my custody just the same as you." Pausing the marshal added, "Anyway, I don't believe you'll need them unless you're found not guilty." He paused once again as if searching his thoughts. "I'll bring them in, but you aren't going to need them in your cell. In fact, I might need to go through them to see if there's anything that might link you to these murders."

"When I found Marty he had his gun out as if he was in a gunfight. It rained so hard any tracks left by anyone else were wiped out completely."

"Now how would I know that, being as you helped yourself to his personals? The papers you say you took off him belonged to his partner Rudy. How do I know you didn't kill them both and wait until this morning when all the tracks were wiped out by last night's storm then ride into town to play innocent, report their murder in an attempt to remove any suspicion, thus allowing you to ride off scot-free?"

Duke hung his head in futility. The marshal already had him pegged as the killer. There was no use arguing with the man, not unless he could think of something to change the lawman's mind. Walking over to the bunk he sat with his back to the wall and propped his head in his hands. He needed to think. There had to be a way out of this.

What about all of the supplies he just purchased? What would happen to them? He was in trouble here unless he could get out of jail in a hurry. Who were the two men that someone wanted them both dead? Had they killed one another? No, that would have been a head on gunfight; they would have been facing each other. How could he have been so stupid? Had he not gone to the Divine Watering Hole for a drink he would not be behind bars right this moment. He would be back on his place by now raising stone walls.

Mother Nature and the devil had sure pulled the plug on Duke Robinson. He didn't for one minute think God had anything to do with the recent turn of events. If anything this had been the work of the devil.

Duke heard a horse clopping by in the mud of the street and he got up to look out his cell window. It was the strange rider he had seen the night before outside of town. He started to yell at the man, but the horse made a right turn and was quickly out of sight. He was wearing the green alligator boots!

The rider had been an old man from the looks of things. His hat was pulled down low over his forehead and his coat drawn tight around him. Around his neck was the customary scarf most western men wore. His boots were identical to the ones in the window at Scranton Lane's mercantile. His pants had covered the tops, but the bottom of his right boot had been fairly visible. Did the strange rider have anything to do with the men's recent demise? It was a possibility. He had seen the man three times now, the first when he'd left the Divine Watering Hole, last night in the middle of the storm, and just now.

The marshal had gone to gather Duke's things and finish his job. No telling when the man would be back. Duke looked through the bars to the man's desk and saw his name on a plaque, Russell Fowler. Unless the marshal found another lead somewhere he would do everything in his power to convict Duke John for murder.

Duke laid his head against the steel bars and closed his eyes. "Lord, please help me," he prayed. At the same moment, he realized all of his troubles were accounted to one decision, the decision to have a drink the day before. Never again would he make that mistake. He swore at that very moment he would ride miles around saloons to avoid them—if he ever got free of his present bonds.

A little after noon the young lady from the café came in to bring him food. She was a sweet young girl, and it bothered Duke she should see him like this, caged up like an old coon.

"I brought you something to eat," she said handing him a plate through the bars.

"Thank you."

"Your name's Duke?"

"Yes ma'am, that's my name."

"Well, I'll give you credit. You sure have got some kind of nerve," she said as she took a seat at the marshal's desk.

"I'm not sure I follow you."

"My name is Brooke Bennett." She paused to let it sink in. "You filed on all Daddy's water rights. You bought Scranton Lane's place up in the hills overlooking Sandstone Lake, you registered the circle R brand with the Stockman Association and you didn't even introduce yourself. Now, what's a girl supposed to think about a man like that?"

"Not much, I reckon."

"Not much is right. Just what did you plan on doing with all them water rights and no cows?" She was fishing for information, but she had a right if her name was Bennett.

Duke looked at her and thought how pretty she was. "It's not what you think."

"Just what am I thinking, you know so much."

Duke knew what folks would suspect. "You're likely thinking I was planning to steal your father's cattle and not even have to move them from one range to another."

"Go on," she said.

"I know what it looks like, but none of it is true. I wasn't going to steal a single cow. I was planning to bring in my own beef."

"How were you going to get your own?"

"There are cattle in the breaks off to the west of my place about fifty miles back in the rough country, I was going to brand some of the wild ones and move them onto my range."

"If there are cattle in them breaks, I bet Daddy doesn't know, and I'll bet they're his anyway."

"Well now, I won't argue with you lass, but..."

"Who are you calling lass? I'm sixteen years old and I'm old enough to take care of myself."

It was clear the young lady was offended.

"I didn't mean to imply you weren't capable. I just meant you were young maybe."

"Maybe, you're the dumbest smart boy I ever did see. Why you've completely outsmarted yourself and now you're going to hang for murder. Young, maybe, but you sure have a lot to learn about girls."

"It doesn't look like I'm going to get the chance," Duke said.

He ate his meal before she could drag the conversation in a direction he didn't want to go. He ate in silence and when he finished she got up and met him at the cell bars. When he handed over his plate he held onto it for a minute and then looked into her eyes. "Do you know an old cowboy who wears dark green alligator boots and rides an appaloosa gelding?"

"No. Why?"

"I saw him last night in the storm when the lightning flashed and a little while ago I saw him ride by my cell window. He may have something to do with the killings."

"Well, I've not seen nor heard the man you're describing, but...she took the plate then and headed out the door. Just as she reached it she paused. "You know, the man you're describing sounds like the old hostler who was killed last year, Moe Rogers. But that's silly; he died over a year ago. His alligator boots are in the front window at Scranton Lane's store."

The young girl stepped out and closed the door behind her. Those boots were exactly the same as the ones the old man on the horse wore. They couldn't possibly be the same pair, unless...

Duke shook his head to get rid of the thought. Nobody comes back from the dead. He jumped up and looked out the window. He couldn't believe his eyes. There was not a single track visible from the old man's horse. In the middle of the muddy ally way, not one single track was left behind. Now he questioned his own sanity. He didn't want to go there.

His thoughts changed to the girl. Well, if she knew about his papers, everyone in town knew about them. He was in deep trouble when he should be building the new ranch house. How long did he have, two weeks, a month? There was no telling how long, but if he didn't find a plausible explanation for what took place, an explanation Marshal Russell Fowler would believe, he was a condemned man. Man? A grown man he had yet to become.

Brooke Bennett. So she was one of the Bennett clan. When she got home the lid was going to blow off sure. All she had to do was ride home explain what was happening to their pa and all the flood waters in China wouldn't hold the old man back. The senior Bennett would saddle up and ride for town. What an introduction that would be!

Chapter 7

A snip of a girl appeared in his life and suddenly the woman Duke wanted to share his life with had form. Funny how being behind bars could make a young man think. Brooke Bennett. But when old man Bennett found out what he was up to his chances with the girl would be ten million to one. Whatever possessed him to try and make such a play? The plan as conceived had been a good one, it still was. He would still be proving up just fine but for the murders of two men. Who could have killed them?

What about the marshal? He knew both men. Could he have disposed of them for some unknown reason while using Duke for the perfect scapegoat?

Someone had killed both men, but who? There was the Bennett ranch, but other than them, you had to ride twenty miles south to reach the McCarver ranch. Of course, there was the circle R, his own brand. Well, he wanted to make a big splash when he arrived. As things stood, he couldn't have made a bigger splash than to be accused of murder on his first trip to town. How could he have been so careless?

The girl was right. He was a bumbling idiot, fairly quick with a shooting iron maybe, but a bumbling idiot as young men go. If there was a way out of this, he had no earthly idea what it might be.

The thought occurred to him. What if he was next? There didn't even have to be a trial. If he was killed the townsfolk would say good riddance to a complete stranger, a murderer and troublemaker.

For the first time, Duke realized the gravity of his situation. He was going to die if he didn't find a way to get out of this cell. He was going to die for something he didn't do and he could expect no one to come to his aid. He didn't have any long-standing friends in this town, he didn't know anyone but for those he'd met in the last twenty-four hours, and such relationships would buy nothing, not even the girl.

He lay back on his bunk and looked up to the ceiling. He could see no way out, yet he had to try something. He looked at the window bars and saw where someone had scraped at them trying to loosen them from their mortar, but further study told him such an approach was of little use. He looked down at the floor and realized he had a wooden floor. How much room would be under the floor once he opened a hole?

Standing he looked out into the street and guessed he had about two feet between the floor and the ground. A good eight to ten inches of that would be taken up by the floor joist. Fourteen inches would be enough, he thought. It would be close, but if he could slip under the floor he might find a way out in the dark of night. Of course, there was the possibility of a snake, maybe even spiders, but if he remained in this cell death was more than just a possibility.

While no one was around he drew out a small knife he carried inside his left boot and pried on the floor. He tried almost every inch before he found a weak spot he might be able to pull up. Slowly and carefully he worked at the wood trying to loosen the boards. It was taking a long time, but as he worked he noticed the wood finally loosened. Then he heard boot steps on the boardwalk outside and he straightened up immediately. He plopped back down on his bunk.

The front door pushed open and for a moment all he saw was the man's looming shadow spread across the floor then he stepped inside closing the door behind him. He walked across the room and dropped most of Duke's belongings in the corner. All but the saddlebags. Those he placed on his desk.

Duke noticed immediately how he felt when the lawman entered the room. Though he was behind bars, he still felt free when he was alone, yet the moment the marshal invaded the office he suddenly felt trapped as if every move he made was being watched and judged. He felt smothered.

Tilting his head Duke watched as the marshal went through his belongings. Such action was a violation of his privacy. The man would soon know everything there was to know about Duke John Robinson. Of course, he'd been going through them already or Brooke Bennett wouldn't have known what she knew.

He squirmed on his bunk and wondered how the marshal would use the information he found to develop a motive, to prove he'd done something he had not. There was enough evidence in his bags to hang him on appearance alone, but appearances could be deceiving. In this case, he was being framed. But the marshal wouldn't care about that.

He watched Fowler closely as he went through the papers in his belongings. Then a thought occurred to him, "Why don't you check my gun. You'll see the only bullet I've fired is the one that I fired yesterday in the saloon and

I haven't cleaned my weapon since. I haven't even reloaded it."

"You don't understand. You've had enough time to fire that gun a hundred times, then clean your weapon and fire one more shot. No, that defense won't do you any good, not now," the marshal said without even looking Duke's way.

Duke hung his head in despair. He was going to hang unless he could escape. The marshal wasn't looking for evidence to clear him; he was looking for evidence to incriminate him further and there was plenty of that in his saddlebags. Marshal Fowler was looking to seal Duke's fate and make a name for himself in the process. Justice for Duke John Robinson appeared to be hanging from the end of a rope.

"You own the old Sagebrush Mine?" the marshal asked.

"Yes sir. Ian and I also own most of the water in the area," Duke explained.

"I noticed. Who is Ian?"

"Ian is my partner, this was all his idea."

"What were your plans? I think now that murder is involved I should know."

"There are a good many wild cattle in the breaks back to the west of Sandstone Lake. We were going to brand a few of them and start our own herd."

"Does Bennett know about this?"

"No, he doesn't." Thinking about the girl he added, "Not yet anyway."

"You can bet your britches he doesn't else he'd be in here dragging you out of my jail to hang you himself. Lane says you already started building."

"Yes, sir. I started up above the lake where I could see out over the whole countryside."

"Why isn't Ian with you?"

"He had some business back home to take care of, so he said."

"Where might that be?"

"I don't know, I didn't ask."

"He's your partner?"

"Yes, sir."

"And you don't have any idea where he is?"

"I didn't figure it was any of my business at the time."

Getting up, Marshal Fowler walked over to the gun cabinet and took down a shotgun broke it open then loaded it. He lay the gun on his desk facing the door. Returning to the cabinet he fished out three rifles and loaded them as well, laying them on the right side of the desk also facing the door, easy to hand. Then he sat back down at his desk and inventoried everything in Duke's saddlebag. Once he finished he neatly put everything back in place. Then he walked over to Duke and held out the list. "Check this and make sure I didn't miss anything."

Duke took the list and figuring nothing missing handed it back, "looks right to me."

"If you're acquitted I want to make sure you get back everything that belongs to you. The important things will be locked up in the safe. I'll have Scranton pick up your supplies and restock his shelves, giving you credit for what you have. If you go free you can stop by and get your belongings back no questions asked. It'll be inventoried just like your saddlebags."

Duke's curiosity ate at him. "What are all the loaded guns for?"

"When Gaylord Bennett rides into town he'll have his men with him. He'll be coming in this afternoon sure. Things might get a little dicey before I'm able to convince him to turn around and go home. He's the bull of the woods around here. Jack and his sister Brooke have already left for home and when Jack tells the old man you've filed on his water, I'm going to have my hands full."

"You think he'll be that mad?" Duke asked nervously.

"I can guarantee it. Son, you don't realize what you've done. Gaylord Bennett moved in here fifteen years ago with a couple of young'ns and a good wife. They worked hard to build a home and all the time the family grew. Gaylord doesn't know much about book learning, but he's right savvy, has more common sense than most men. Now just when things are finally starting to look good for the Bennett family, you show up with the legal rights to his water. I'm going to try and reason with him, but I'll be honest. If it comes to a shooting affair, I'll let him have you. I'm not going to kill a good man like Gaylord Bennett or one of his men just to hold onto you. If I lose control of them, you're going to have to handle things on your own."

Duke swallowed hard. "How much time you figure I have?"

"If they ride straight in, two maybe three hours, if they talk first, I figure sundown. If they don't come in 'til sundown, things will be a might tougher. Gaylord will have his riders primed for a fight."

"I'm supposed to fight the whole ranch?"

"No, you'll fight Gaylord. He measures out about two of you so the fight won't last long," Fowler said. "I've seen him fight for his land with bigger, tougher men than you.

He'll fight fair if you can call fighting a giant of a man fair."

Duke was getting a queasy feeling in his stomach just thinking about such a fight. "What do you mean by giant?"

"Bennett is six foot seven or eight but he's not just tall, when you see him you'll think he's a grizzly standing upright on two feet."

Why hadn't Ian Durant told him more about the man? He just said old man Bennett was a pushover, getting soft with years. Now the marshal was giving him a completely different description of the man. If Gaylord Bennett was six foot seven, such information would have been useful. Had Ian left out such important details on purpose?

Duke wondered why Ian hadn't attempted filing on the land himself if it was so easy. Ian had provided just enough information to leave Duke holding the bag. Now as he thought about the situation things became clear. Ian was a coward or a very smart tactician. He wanted the land, he wanted the cattle, but he wanted someone else to do all the work and the fighting! Ian would come riding in to pick up the pieces once the bullets stopped flying. Duke swore under his breath knowing full well he was being used.

The sudden realization left him fuming. He'd walked right into a trap and like a dumb farm boy he'd taken the bait. The ramifications were simple. In Dead Woman Crossing he was everyone's enemy. Once he was hung for murder, or hung on general principles what would happen to his papers? Who would get his deeds and his claim? His partner Ian would get everything! He had no family as far as Duke knew, yet Ian knew the entire play. He would get everything as his name was on the papers.

Duke realized he was pacing back and forth in his cell and took a seat. The marshal had him all worked to a frazzle. He could do nothing one way or another, not without the marshal handing him over and if that happened he wouldn't live to see tomorrow. Lying back on his bunk he put his hands behind his head and tried to calm down. The Bennett's would be riding by now.

Brook Bennett was a girl he liked. The girl was sweet and carried herself well. Did she have an older sister or was she the oldest? Duke ran his conversation with Ian through his head and decided she was the oldest, there were two little ones between two and ten. The boys were spread out, Jackson being the oldest. He was placing them in his head, but a lot of good it would do him now. He would be lucky to see another sunrise in Oklahoma Territory.

"I'm going out onto the porch and wait for them there. If they get past me, you're on your own." Marshal Fowler didn't wait for a reply. He opened the door and stepped out onto the boardwalk with his shotgun and the loaded rifles then closed the jailhouse door behind him. Duke waited to hear the footfalls indicating he'd taken a seat on the bench then swiftly jumped to his feet.

Pulling his knife he began to dig and pull while he mumbled, "When I see that Ian I'm going to punch him right in the mouth."

In a few minutes, he had several boards near the back wall up and had pulled his bed out away from it. Carefully he stacked the pulled boards up along the wall so they would blend in with the floor itself hoping the hole would not be noticeable behind his bunk. He would not have time to move the bunk back against the wall if the door opened unexpectedly.

Most of the nails had been loosened, but there were a few that had not and when he tried to pull them they started to squeal telling on his efforts. He only had two maybe three boards left. To get this close and come away empty-handed was not what he wanted. He would still have to dig underneath the outer wall once he was under the floor. It didn't seem possible there would be enough time unless he went down now, but the hole wasn't big enough. Slowly he pried and pulled but his hands and arms made for sad leverage. The boards either wouldn't release, or they gave all at once creating a distinct squeal.

Finally, Duke realized there were horses coming down the street and not just a few. He ripped and tore at the floor then plunged beneath the jailhouse floor into darkness. He was near the back wall already so when he saw a ray of light he went straight for it on his back scooting and pushing along in the dirt. Someone had made this attempt before, the hole was half dug out from the inside already.

The horses stopped and he could hear men talking, but he could not make out what was being said. His time was up! He dug at the partially opened hole with fierce abandon. He felt his knife hit rock a time or two, but kept digging out around it. Eventually, he had a ten-inch hole opened up, but nowhere near big enough to slip his body through. It seemed there was rock on either side, but he kept at it and when one of the rocks dislodged from its mooring, he shoveled more dirt. Still, the hole wasn't big enough.

The difficulty was lying on his back. If he could get on his hands and knees the hole would already be opened up, but the awkward position from which he had to dig left him aching. He could still hear the men talking, but he never let up.

Finally, the hole opened to little more than a foot deep and he made his attempt. Just as he began to wiggle into the hole he heard the jailhouse door open and a yell went up. He got his hands above him against the outer wall and pushed and pulled his body through. He almost stuck at the knees but he was able to twist around and pull himself free.

He sprang from the back side of the jailhouse into the livery stable. His horses were there. Not taking the time to saddle up he opened the gate grabbed a handful of mane and jumped astride his best horse. Bullets whizzed by his ear for a moment and then he was gone. Diving down into Devil's Bend he rode swiftly for about three hundred yards. He came up the other side at a point where a wash emptied into the bend. He took it straight away toward the west, never looking over his shoulder and kept his head down. His horse was fresh and it could run. With no saddle, he was lighter. They'd never catch him this side of Sunday.

Duke rode like the wind, with an occasional pistol shot behind him that was nowhere near its target. Glancing over his shoulder he could see the riders spreading out behind him, yet all of them were coming his way, the Bennett's with Marshal Fowler bringing up the rear.

If a noose they had for him, it swung empty on this night. Before Duke, the land unraveled serene and wild. He kept to the low places. Soon darkness and cold descended. The lineback dun wanted his head and Duke was just about to let him have it when he realized he needed to circle the town and go back for his saddle and bridle. Would the marshal know? Would he be lying in wait for just such a move? Without question, he was going to need his rigging.

Looking back as he crested the knoll he had a good half mile lead, but he needed more. He needed a bigger gap before he could head back toward town.

Without hesitation, he turned the horse to the distant hills and swung a wide circle around the first two, then made a beeline toward Dead Woman Crossing. They would miss him. If they had ridden home to wait for the morrow, they would still miss him. His only worry was Marshal Fowler. Russell Fowler was not the kind of man to take a jailbreak lightly. He would insist on getting his man. He would be coming like a slow and dedicated bloodhound on the trail. He'd been embarrassed by a whelp of a kid, and the town would soon be laughing at him unless he brought Duke in quickly.

Duke didn't want to be anywhere near town, yet it was where he had to ride. As he crossed Devil's Bend he rode up to the small stable behind the jail jumped down and grabbed his harness. He put it on the horse and then placed his saddle blanket and saddle. He pulled the cinch tight, double-checked everything and stepped into the saddle just as the Bennett's cleared the far rise. There was no time to grab anything else. He bolted through town then scurried out the other side of Devil's Bend headed east. He needed distance, and his horse was still fresh.

Chapter 8

Duke's horse carefully searched out each placement of its hooves as the pair navigated the trail leading back to town. A cold shiver ran down the back of Duke's neck, reminding him how close he'd come to being strung up just a few hours ago. At the bottom of the hill, he turned at a right angle toward the south and slipped down into Devils Bend. Two hundred yards through the creek bed he dismounted leaving his horse to graze on some spear grass. Then he eased up the side of the wash to view the situation confronting him.

Somehow he had to recover his personal belongings, but how? How could he ride into a town as well-defended as Dead Woman Crossing and expect to ride out on his own accord when everyone in the country was surely looking for him? That he had managed such a feat earlier that day was encouraging, but to get the rest of his things he would be at much greater risk of waking someone, namely Marshal Russell Fowler. Such an attempt might also require a daylight raid. On this evening, Duke determined the risk was simply too great.

Riding back the way he'd come he navigated a small shale rock slide and climbed out of Devil's Bend. Once he was back in his hiding place he dismounted and tied off his horse. He pulled the saddle and laid the blanket out so he could get some rest. The sun would wake him in the morning. He needed to hang around long enough to see if there wasn't a way to get into town after his personals. He needed his guns and his saddlebags. If nothing else he needed those two items. He would be completely defenseless without his guns, and his saddlebags contained the entire ranch plan. Who was he kidding? It had been Ian's plan all along. He was nothing more than a patsy, a body to take the blame!

"When I see you, you're gonna get it," he mumbled to no one.

At daybreak, he awoke and saddled the dun. No one in town was going to welcome him, but he had to retrieve his things. He might end up right back in jail, but if he did he would have at least tried. He had ridden to the east last evening and placed himself in the direct path of the rising sun, giving him the cover he needed in the early morning hours.

Duke watched from his hillside hideout and looked for any chance to get into the jail after his things. It was noon before he saw his chance. Marshal Fowler left the jail. He watched as the marshal entered the café for lunch when he should have been looking for an escaped prisoner.

Riding down the long hill he crossed the wash and led his horse into the stable behind the jail. Tying off the animal he glanced around, wary of any eyes that might be watching. Satisfied there weren't any he slipped along the south side of the jailhouse opposite where he broke out. At the front of the building, he held up and gave the town a once over. No one was moving about much today so he scurried around to the front door and ducked inside.

There was a man in his former cell working to repair the damage he'd done and both of them were caught by surprise. Duke ran to the gun rack and pulled his pistol, aiming at the carpenter. "Don't make a sound and you won't get hurt."

"What's your name, son?"

"Duke Robinson."

"You don't look like much of a killer to me," the man said.

"I'm not, but I've no time for conversation," Duke added as he buckled on his gun belt, picked up his rifle and saddlebag, thankful they were not locked in the corner safe.

"You're right cautious, but not afraid to take a risk. I like that," the carpenter said.

"Tell Marshal Fowler I didn't kill anyone. I'm not about to hang for something I didn't do."

"I'll tell him, but he sure is going to be mad you coming in here like this and taking things."

"Tell him I'm going to help him solve the murders," Duke said and he slipped out the door with his belongings.

He ran behind the building, stuffed his rifle in the scabbard, tied his saddlebag in place and mounted up. He hit the saddle and spurred his horse to an all-out run. Once out the other end of Devil's Bend, he took a different route away from town in case anyone was waiting for him to return to his former hiding place.

It was pushing sundown when he rode up to his ranch building still under construction. He moved with caution. Someone had been here. His rock piles had been moved some and stacked nearer the house. Looking around he found several small boot prints indicating the intruder had likely been a girl. Nothing was amiss, only someone had been here and for some unknown reason or another, they had helped.

Now, who would do such a thing? Duke wondered as he removed his hat. Taking a closer look at his cover he pulled his hat brush from his saddlebag and brushed it good while he could still see. Setting it aside he unsaddled his horse and made his bed in the interior of the building site. He picketed the horse there as well. Lying back against his saddle he wondered who was trying to frame him. Was the marshal involved? Not likely, but who? Who had killed Rudy and Marty and what about the bank robbery last year that got the town hostler killed? Who was pulling the strings?

Just then he saw the old cowboy, the one with alligator boots, sitting across the lake on his horse. Could it be him? He thought for a moment then got up and placed his saddle blanket on the dun. It was time he had a conversation with the old fellow. When he turned to look at the old man he was gone. Duke shivered and let the blanket slide back to the ground. Who was the man and how could he disappear so quickly?

The carpenter had apparently gone right back to work repairing the jailhouse floor, showing little concern for Duke. He was installing set screws so no one could just pull the floor up again without the proper tools. Who was the man? Why hadn't he run to the marshal immediately? Maybe he figured the marshal would bring Duke in one way or another. It stood to reason. Surely Marshal Fowler would be riding this way already. The new ranch house would be the first place Fowler would look. While he might rest here for a few hours, Duke knew he would have to move out before sunup. His new home would be in the outlying hills and breaks west of the ranch. He would have to move like a ghost leaving little to no tracks. Such thoughts brought him back to the old man. Who was he, and how did he disappear so easily?

When he awoke stars were high overhead. He looked at them long enough to guess it was about three in the morning. Getting up he quickly saddled the lineback dun and rode away in the dark. He knew where he was headed and he picked up his branding iron. He was headed for the breaks off to the west. There were unbranded cattle back there and he was going to start building his herd. Of course, the Bennett's would know about the cattle by now, but it was no matter. He had to try.

There was the Sagebrush Mine, but the marshal knew about that place too. He would check everywhere and he would eventually end up in the breaks. Duke scowled for there seemed nowhere for him to hole up. Not that he wanted to, but folks would be out looking for him. Would the marshal regroup and bring a fresh posse? It would be good to know what he was dealing with.

The trail widened out before him as the sun lightened the sky behind him to a dull gray. He passed Bennett cattle early on but kept riding, checking his surroundings every few minutes. He could not afford to have anyone to sneak up on him.

Maybe the marshal didn't leave town until first light. That would give him a good head start, but if Fowler left yesterday he would be coming right along. The marshal would not be amused. Duke understood what he had done to the man. He embarrassed him in front of the entire town. He would have to bring Duke in; otherwise, Fowler was through being marshal at Dead Woman Crossing.

Not only had he escaped, but he had ridden back into town in broad daylight and gathered his things. Such a story would spread fast in this part of Oklahoma and Marshal Fowler would be laughed at by friend and foe alike. That is why the situation could not be allowed to stand. Fowler needed to salvage his reputation provided he still had one. Whether or not Marshal Fowler had possessed a reputation beforehand, Duke had no way of knowing, yet he certainly had one now and folks would be amused, but not Fowler. Duke remembered the wanted poster for Black Bart and smiled. Folks were already laughing at Fowler, and not because of him.

What was the old English rhyme? "When I did well, I heard it never. When I did ill, I heard it ever!" Duke spoke the rhyme to no one, but the saying of it put an exclamation mark on how he felt at the moment.

So they would come, but from where and when? Who would ride with the marshal or would he come alone? Certainly, a few of the Bennett's would have a vested interest in seeing him brought to justice. What would Brooke say to that? Would she say anything at all? Were the boot tracks he'd witnessed at the home site hers?

He rode warily, keeping an eye wandering in all directions for he knew not the country the way local folks would know it and this in itself was a disadvantage.

There on a far hill to his north sat the rider. It was the old man he'd witnessed the night before, the night of the murders, the same old horse, the same boots, the same everything. Those boots were a dead ringer for the ones in the window at Scranton Lane's store. Without thinking he turned his horse to ride over and confront the old timer, yet when he completed his turn around the big rock, the old man was gone.

Duke halted his horse, startled. There was no place the old man could have hid, not even behind a tree, but he was gone just as if he'd never existed. He had to get out of the area. He looked over the ground where he saw the old man, but nothing gave any indication anyone had been there.

The man had simply disappeared in between glances, leaving Duke with a very uneasy feeling. Where did he go? From where Duke sat there was nowhere the man *could* have gone. So where was he?

Duke nudged his mount and continued on. Marshal Fowler would be coming like a hound dog on the trail, but who else would ride? That bothered Duke more than anything. If he had to defend himself against the Bennett's it meant he would never have a chance with Brooke. The thought rankled.

There was another old saying Duke remembered that said, "Tis strange but true, the truth is always strange."

Believing the statement to be true, where should he start looking? Someone had killed those men, but who and why? It would be in a strange answer, an unsuspecting one he thought. It could be anyone, but who would do such a thing? Who would want the men dead? What about the old man who had just disappeared?

First, a former Texas Ranger had been killed at the time of the bank robbery one year ago and now Marty Jones and Rudy Tallmadge were dead. That Duke was a suspect in the recent killings he could understand, but who killed Moe Rodgers? The bank robbers of course, but the question remained, who were they?

As he neared the breaks he scanned ahead to choose his path in. Satisfied he had found one he neared the entrance and pulled rein while he sat staring. The tracks before him indicated someone was here ahead of him. One lone horse, its stride indicated a big one. The size of the hoof prints indicated the same thing. The horse and man made for a heavy pair. Was it old man Bennett?

From where he sat he could see the opening to Sage Brush mine. As he looked up he saw a flash coming from the entrance and a white-hot burning sensation ripped through his upper torso lifting him from the saddle. His horse took off running back the way it had come leaving Duke lying in the wide open spaces where he could be finished off by the shooter with no trouble. The shot had come from the mine entrance nearly five hundred yards away.

At the risk of being shot again, Duke lay perfectly still. He was hurt bad he knew, but he still had his pistols. His idea was to draw the shooter in close and let him have it if he was still alive by then. He lay with his eyes closed and tried not to hyperventilate in a panic. This was the hardest thing because it was contrary to everything his mortal body was telling him to do. Good shooting, but Duke wasn't dead yet.

The pain was unbearable, and in time Duke passed out. When he came to he had no idea how long he'd been unconscious, but the sky was much the same dull gray. He dare not risk moving or looking about. The shooter had not moved in to finish him off or he would be dead. If the man was still out there lurking, Duke would give away his advantage if he moved. He had lost a lot of blood and he was weak from the loss, but he could not move, not until night overtook them. How many hours would that be? If the man was still out there and he moved now he was as good as dead. The fact he was still alive was no small miracle.

How could anyone endure such pain and remain among the living? Just breathing took its toll. He was two hundred yards from any cover. The shooter would have all the advantage even in the darkness. Darkness! Duke realized suddenly it was getting dark. He'd been unconscious all day. Why hadn't the man moved in and finished him off? The fact he was down and hadn't moved should have drawn the man who ambushed him in. Duke was puzzled. He should have moved in once he saw there was no movement from Duke, but this man, whoever he was had shown no such inclination. If he'd moved at all he'd ridden off in another direction. Why hadn't the man finished the job? Then it hit him. The shooter thought he'd killed him. He'd managed to lie so still it had fooled whoever it was into thinking he was dead.

He knew very well where he was. He didn't need to open his eyes and look around. He was lying in the open field about two hundred yards from the entrance to the breaks, five hundred yards from the mine. He was out in the wide open and he'd been shot. The bullet had entered just under his left collarbone and lodged under his left shoulder. The pain was getting worse. Where was his horse? Surely it wouldn't have run very far. The dun as good as they come. He would stay with his rider, so where was he? Duke listened carefully and soon he picked out the sound of his horse cropping grass in the near distance. So he was still here. He had a chance.

Suddenly he wondered if he could move once darkness set in. Was he so bad off he wouldn't be able to move? He had no idea. He couldn't chance a test maneuver for if the gunman was watching he'd be shot again. He had to lay still and continue playing possum. His left shoulder burned as if it was on fire and icy cold fingers of death pulled at his chest. He didn't figure he had a punctured lung because he was able to breathe slowly and control his intake of oxygen, but he was hurt bad. How bad he had no idea. When he moved he would surely start bleeding again provided he'd ever stopped. He could count on that. How much blood did he have left? Such a question he could not answer. If he stayed where he was he would die, the buzzards would have him by morning, then he remembered, maybe even a particular cat.

Well after dark Duke opened his eyes and lifted his head. He looked up to see the old man with dark green boots as he squatted by a reflecting firelight with his back to him. The man seemed to have something on his back, wings?

"Oh that's just great," Duke mumbled, "now I'm seeing things."

The old man turned to look at him, squinted his eyes and smiled. Forcing himself, Duke pushed up onto his right elbow saw the bandage wrapping his left shoulder and then passed out again.

"Pilgrim, you are more trouble to watch over than an entire herd of cattle." A minute later the old timer picked Duke up and placed him in his saddle with ease, his horse stood stock still sensing that his rider was hurt. Taking Duke's new rope, the strange old man tied him in place so he could not fall off while traveling. Taking up the reins, the suspicious looking old fellow in green alligator boots led him down the trail.

Each step the lineback dun took jarred Duke's shoulder, yet the boy remained unconscious. There was a bullet in him that had to come out. There was only one ranch nearby, and that's where Duke's guardian headed now. The only place close enough was the Bennett ranch and it was a good twelve miles on the north side of Peace Valley Range.

Slowly they made their way through the long valley toward the Bennett holdings. They were riding on the wide open range under the cover of darkness. Town would be another fifteen to twenty miles and the boy would never make a ride of that distance.

If the boy could hang on until he reached the Bennett place he had a chance. Of course, the Bennett family might just as well let him die once they discovered who he was, but the old timer believed they would do the right thing. He simply had nowhere else to deliver the young man where he might get the help he needed.

He held the horses to a slow pace so as not to jar the young man more than necessary, but eventually, he had to stop and secure the boy again. How long did he have before the boy would pass the point of no return? He wanted to do more to help, but he hadn't the time, not if he was to save the boy's life. Besides, there was only so much a Guardian Angel assigned to a case was allowed to do.

Glancing down, the old man realized there was blood all over the young man's saddle. Duke would no doubt be upset about the blood, but he'd no choice but to tie the boy to his saddle. Moe, as he'd been called while on earth, knew if the young man fell from his horse the fall would likely finish him and his services as Guardian Angel would no longer be needed. Duke Robinson was his first assignment and failure was not an option.

Finally, they topped over a rise and he saw the lights of the ranch house in the distance. It was only one light, but there was light. Then while Moe was focusing on the light someone turned out the lamp. Someone was still up.

Nudging his horse forward he held onto the boy's reins and made his way down to the ranch house. As he rode up to the front porch he stepped down, untied the boy then laid him by the door. After rapping on the door he stepped into his saddle and rode away leaving the dun reins tied to the hitching post.

It was up to the Bennett family to save the young man now. A Guardian Angel could not interfere in one's destiny beyond certain limits. Had he been better at his job, had more experience, the boy would have never been shot in the first place. Because of his inexperience, Duke's fate was now left to mortal man.

Duke rolled his eyes and tried to sit up just in time to see the old man riding away, yet he was seeing things, unexplainable things like wings on the man's back. At this point, he was more dead than alive. He tried to yell but no sound came. Again he tried, this time from farther down in his chest still nothing came of his attempt. With despair, he realized he had no voice. The bullet wound had stolen his ability to speak, for now, or forever he did not know.

Slowly he struggled to sit up against the front door and collapsed back on the porch. He tried to rise again but couldn't. He was struggling just to think. What was happening? Was he dying? If he wasn't he was as close as he ever wanted to be. He lay where he was for a few minutes and then began to crawl.

With all the gumption he had remaining he pulled himself up into a chair on the front porch. Someone inside was stirring. With his last bit of energy, he rapped as loudly as he could against the front window pane. He heard a faint stirring inside the house and then once again he blacked out.

Duke was not conscious to witness the presence of Brooke, her mother and several other members of the Bennett family as they gathered around him on the front porch.

Chapter 9

Duke could hear the comings and goings in the room around him. He was in someone's bed but he couldn't move and he did not want to see. What happened? Where was he? He couldn't remember. How bad was he hurt? He tried to move his lips to speak but nothing happened. Nothing he tried worked. Someone was in the room with him, but how could he get their attention? Finally, he blacked out again.

When he came to, he heard footsteps somewhere near him. Whoever it was seemed to be walking on a wooden floor. The person was very light-footed, barefoot even. He tried to open his eyes and suddenly he realized they were already open for they blinked. His vision was so blurred he couldn't see. He could hear goings on around him, but he couldn't respond in any way shape or form. Then he remembered the concussion of the bullet to his left shoulder. He sighed and closed his eyes. He'd been shot. He could no longer speak and no longer see.

How bad off was he? His condition couldn't be good, yet he was alive for the time being. His shoulder was on fire.

Where was he? Who had given up their bed for him? The room smelled of perfume, and cinnamon, what was going on? Then he heard a faint swish from a dress as it swept by his bed. Who was in the room with him? It surely wasn't the gruff looking old man with wings who had dropped him on the doorstep. No one was talking. Shouldn't there be voices? What was this place, purgatory?

Someone was rubbing his forehead with a washcloth and he opened his eyes. He looked up into the eyes of Brooke Bennett and she smiled.

"Well, there you are. We were beginning to wonder if you were ever coming back."

His lips fumbled the words. "How long have I been here?"

"Three days, but you needed to heal. Doc said your gunshot wound was the nastiest bullet hole he ever saw in a man, let alone a boy. It tore you up real good. Then you must have hit your head on a rock when you fell off your horse," she said.

"Thank you for being here. I would not have enjoyed waking up before a complete stranger."

Brooke blushed. "Well, I'm not much more than that."

Duke looked about the room and saw his saddlebags sitting in the corner along with his rifle and gun belt. He saw his clothes neatly placed and realized he was currently without them. Feeling a bit embarrassed he looked back to Brook and tried to smile. "I guess I did things up real good, didn't I."

"Well, you have made folks stand up and take notice, especially Daddy. He said that bullet would have killed most men. Marshal Fowler says you still belong to him just as soon as you can ride." The girl was treating him a bit nicer than he remembered the last time they spoke.

"I didn't kill those men."

"You're going to have to prove that to the marshal," she said.

Duke looked about the room again. This time he took it all in. He noticed the interior walls were log cabin style along with the roof. The floor was a dark walnut anyone would be proud of. The one window in the room was graced by a rather detailed light green curtain. There were a dresser and chest of drawers and a nightstand next to the bed. There were a few dolls in the room and Duke looked back at Brook.

"You're room?" he asked.

"Not for the last three days."

"Where have you been sleeping?"

"My little sister's room, don't worry, you have my room for as long as you need it."

Duke tried to sit up, but pain shot through every portion of his body and he dropped back onto the bed compressing the feather pillow. "That might be a while," he admitted.

"You aren't ready to start moving around yet," Brooke said as she peeled back the blanket to look at his bandage. You're bleeding again. I have to go get Momma so we can change this bandage. We had this stopped so don't try to move anymore," she ordered and left the room.

He lay still as ordered and looked around the girl's room. If she kept her room this nice, what could she do with a home of her own he wondered. Then he remembered who he was and where he came from. No girl in her right mind would want to spend the rest of her life with the likes of Duke John Robinson. Suddenly his thinking was sober. He had to be crazy to think he could pull off such a deal as he'd planned. Actually, full credit for this idea could go to Ian. Even if someone else didn't want him dead, the Bennett's would surely have an ax to grind, and where did he find himself?

Who pulled the trigger and shot him? Was it one of the Bennett boys or how about old man Bennett himself? He had witnessed the tracks made by a big horse carrying a big man. The old man would not like what Duke had done at all. While he had never met the elder Bennett, it was a certainty he would not take the news well that his water rights had been filed on by a couple of wet-behind-the-ears kids. Now one of those kids was lying in his daughter's bed and had been for the last three days. The fact he would meet the elder Bennett was certain, the question was when, and how would the old man treat him? Looking around it bothered Duke that he had tried to play his cards at all. He didn't want to displace these people. Not a single one.

Duke heard the hurried footsteps coming down the hall and Brooke returned with her mother who was carrying more bandage material.

"Well young man, Brooke tells me you are awake. How do you feel?"

He looked into the hazel eyes of a strong-willed woman who would no doubt run her house the way Mr. Bennett ran his ranch. Bennett might own the entire countryside, but when he set foot inside his own doors he was apt to receive orders from his wife. She ran the household and there was no mistake about it.

"I feel like I've been trampled by a stampede," he said.

"I'd say you described just about what happened. Don't you know you're supposed to duck once the bullets start flying?" She laid the bandages on the nightstand beside the bed and started sorting out what she needed.

"I would have, only I didn't hear the report of the rifle until the bullet hit me." Duke started to sit up.

"Lay still," Brooke admonished. Pushing him back into place she held him motionless. "I told you not to move, you're going to aggravate your wound and make it bleed more."

"I'm not a prisoner, am I? I'd like to sit up."

Mrs. Bennett looked on and offered in a straight forward business-like manner, "Actually you are a prisoner. Marshal Fowler said you are to be brought to him just as soon as we are able to move you."

"Brook, help him to sit up and I'll re-bandage him like we've been doing."

Brooke got her hands under Duke's back and helped him to sit up straight although the pain was almost unbearable. He knew they were doing what they had to do. Brooke helped to hold him still once he was upright and Mrs. Bennett went to work changing the bandage.

"You haven't been much company," she commented.

"Well ma'am, I've sort of been laid up."

"I figured as much. Doc Draper said to feed you just as soon as you could eat, but to take it mighty slow, otherwise, you're liable to upset everything he's done so far."

Mrs. Bennett finished her unwrapping of the old bandage and applied the new one. "You realize you're going to have to marry my daughter," she said as she wrapped. "You sleeping in her bed and all, folks are already beginning to talk."

Duke turned ghost white as he looked into Brooke's eyes and suddenly both of the Bennett women busted out laughing. Duke, on the other hand, didn't see anything funny in her comment.

Mrs. Bennett never stopped wrapping his wound. "I can see you're not used to being around much laughter. We'll have to break you in," the elder Bennett said. "There now, Brooke, help him lay back down while I get rid of these nasty old bandages."

Brooke helped him do as her mother said and suddenly he realized he was nowhere near ready to get out of bed. The pain was now coming at him from all directions. Brooke realized Duke's dilemma almost immediately and gave him a glass of water.

"Here, you're dehydrated. You need water and this is the only thing you can drink for now."

Duke looked down at his now gangly form and no longer recognized what he saw. He laid his head back in despair. The shooter had robbed him of a good deal of his livelihood even if he survived this ordeal. Who had it been? Who wanted him dead? He could now pass easily for a skeleton to be hung out on All Hallows' Eve. Well, his rations of late had been a big contributor. He hadn't been eating like he should.

Mrs. Bennett returned with a small bowl of beef stew and Brooke took it from her. "I'll feed him, Mama."

"All right, but I don't want any shenanigans going on in here," she replied as she let go of the bowl. She then moved about the room to straighten a few things like a picture on the wall and a runner on the dresser and the vase had to be placed just right. She had been watching the two young people interact from the corner of her eye. Once satisfied she left the room.

"Your mother is a cautious woman," Duke observed.

"She has a lot invested in me. She just wants to make sure things go well for you," Brooke said as she spooned another bite of stew into Duke's mouth. His third bite and his fourth would be the bottom of the bowl. Duke looked on in amazement as the girl scraped the bottom to get everything on the spoon.

"That's all I get?"

Brook shoved the final spoonful of stew into Duke's slack-jawed mouth and said, "For now. We have to ration your intake according to Doc Draper's orders, otherwise, we risk losing you." Smiling she added. "I'd like to keep you around for a while."

In the window outside sat the man on his horse, the one who had brought Duke to the Bennett homestead. Duke's eyes bulged causing Brooke to turn and look.

"Do you see something?"

"Don't you?"

"No, I don't see a thing."

Duke laid his head back and closed his eyes. Suddenly he was tired. He felt out of place. The room he was in didn't fit, his shoulder hurt something awful, and now his stomach was rumbling. After only a couple of bites, his stomach now had a life of its own. Must be the fact he hadn't eaten in three or four days and not much the three previous weeks. And what about the old man in the window? Who was he? Couldn't anyone else see him?

For a moment Duke opened his eyes and looked out the window. Nothing, nobody was there. He closed his eyes and lay back again. It was unsettling, such a thing as this.

Chapter 10

Charlie Bolton was playing poker in the Divine Watering Hole along with Marshal Russell Fowler who was growing suspicious of the man before him. While he knew about Black Bart, he didn't know Charlie Bolton and he was one and the same man. Also in the game sat Claude Peppers who owned the local butcher shop. The game was a spirited one and designed to keep Fowler off the street for a few hours. The town marshal had no idea of the proceedings which were about to take place in his own town and could do nothing to stop them had he known.

The boardwalk across the street was a cool place to rest in the shade and Captain Adam Carter, a stranger to Dead Woman Crossing, occupied the well-worn bench outside the marshal's office. Captain Carter was a slick dressed man in black and white. He dressed in black from head to toe, but for his white fringe shirt. If there was dust on anything he wore, it was not recognizable. He kept himself that clean.

He studied the town with care. He had been watching the comings and goings of the people in town and he saw nothing that alarmed him. The Crossing was as warm a town as a body could find west of St. Louis. Everyone waved or offered hello and those who didn't, tipped their hat or smiled, and nodded their head in greeting.

Carter was a tall young man with almost black hair. He had an enviable smile which came easy to his lips, deep blue eyes, and smooth skin. He wore no facial hair and kept himself neatly shaven. Every morning his last act before a mirror was to splash on some Thompson's Wild Cherry phosphate. While most everyone in the country used it as a spiritual medicine, he preferred the smell enough to use the liquid as an aftershave, an idea he had come up with himself. The price of three bottles for forty-five cents made the concoction a perfect travel companion and though often asked, he never revealed his secret.

Women rarely failed to take a second look and sometimes when their eyes met his, their hearts fluttered and skipped a few beats, a detail Captain Carter was completely unacquainted with. He had the idea women appeared to be fond of him, but that was all.

The town he observed at noontide was bustling with people. Three buckboards and a number of freight wagons, the just arrived noon stage, and the company man preparing it for departure. This involved unhitching the tired team and replacing the worn out mules with fresh animals. Most of the hitch rails were dotted with brands of every type lining the street on this day.

Carter, conscious someone now stood beside him was startled. Aware he was no longer alone he looked up at the young man who was scarcely more than a boy. He had deep brown eyes and a shock of hair that needed the attention of a good barber. "Captain Carter, I presume?" he paused. "William Sanderson sent me to fetch you. My name is Kid Bradley."

"Have you got a last name," Carter paused in order to get his answer.

The kid patted the bone handle pair with his agile fingertips. "Not since I strapped these guns on."

Carter noticed both tied down guns and felt his self-assured manner slipping away. Just what was he getting himself into? He got to his feet and looked the package over. Kid Bradley was no more than seventeen and a good foot shorter than him, but those guns the kid wore would not know such a thing. The weapons were capable of killing and probably already had. The kid wore a light blue and white checkered long sleeve shirt, a tan vest and dark brown boots with his too long jeans folded at the bottom.

"Sanderson is waiting for us," he reminded the captain.

"Oh yes, we mustn't keep the man waiting," Carter said. He smiled and thrust out his open hand. "Nice to know you, kid. Are you working for Sanderson?"

"Bradley's eyes shone with faint humor, "I work for no man. I work with him." The statement was flat and unconditional.

"I see."

As the two of them walked, the captain noted that there was something off balance in the young man's personality. A disturbing trait he could not quite put his finger on, but given time he would figure out what was different about Kid Bradley. Whatever the problem was, it effectively placed Adam on edge. He was alert as never before in the young man's presence. "Where is Sanderson?"

"He's down at the bank. He said to walk down here and see if you were in town yet. If you were he wanted you to wait for him down at the hotel. He'll be right along."

The two men entered the hotel lobby and then went through the French doors into the dining room. They took a seat at the corner window and Carter pulled out a fresh cigar. Lighting it he settled back into his seat and looked across the table at the kid.

"Who all is in town," he asked in order to keep the conversation going.

"A fellow named Charles Bolton's playing cards with Marshal Fowler, Clay Allison, and Black Jack Ketchum is down to the Divine Watering Hole tying one on. He's pure meanness when he's been drinking, which seems to be all the time."

"With hands like that around, what does Sanderson need me for?"

"I don't rightly know, but he said you were the man for the job. Said you'd stack up against the best of them. I'm sort of wondering myself." Bradley's grin was distorted just enough to let Carter know the kid did not believe he was capable.

What distinguishing trait did the kid possess that made him so disconcerting? Was he missing something? Not the two guns, for Carter had seen two tied down guns many times before. No, there was something else, some feature in the young man's personality that as yet went unnoticed. Whatever it was, Captain Carter was certain that once triggered the trait would reveal the lurking menace that was Kid Bradley.

"Sanderson's hired some good men. You'll be working with the best." Kid Bradley offered after a moment of silence. "Picked up a few more today. Ian Durant may be one of the best. He's a tough and capable hombre. Knows more about guns and how to use them as anybody I ever saw. Three more came in behind him, Poindexter, Fredrickson, and Jenkins."

From the manner in which the kid spoke those names carried a lot of weight with him, but they fell on the deaf ears of Captain Adam Carter.

"Do you believe they will fight?"

"That bunch?" Bradley turned and noted the crowd. "They'll fight. That Circle B outfit has some cagy old wolves who fought in the war and they've been fighting Indians ever since. They don't scare worth a hoot. They ain't gun shy and on Saturday night they like to play hard. That's where we'll get them."

"You mean brace them when they're drunk."

Kid Bradley didn't like the accusation. He felt pinned and Carter saw the look in his eyes when he said it. The kid was insane! The only thing that mattered to him was his reputation with a gun. He wouldn't care one wit how he got his reputation, as long as he got one. For a moment Carter thought the boy was actually going to draw on him.

"Sanderson says you can fight," the kid said easing the tension between them.

"I do all right. I was six years in the army if that means anything at all. Four of those years were on the Mississippi during the war. I served aboard the Ironclad *Essex*."

"Then you spent a great deal of time in Baton Rouge."

"How could you possibly know that? I've not told anyone where I served."

"I was born and raised just outside of Baton Rouge. The *Essex* was docked there throughout much of the war. When the war was over I made my way to St. Louis and spent a year there. Having been orphaned by the war, I started to travel."

"So you're one of them Gaslight Boys what used to roam the city streets looking for trouble."

"Now you know who I am, but I'm still a little shy on knowledge of you. Ever been west before now?" the kid asked.

"I was born in the west just a few years before the gold fever of forty-nine. When war broke out I was seventeen. I signed on with a bunch from Southern California and stayed in a few years after the war fighting the Apache."

The kid seemed to have his appetite for questions quenched for the time being. "Sanderson speaks very highly of you, but he's only one piece of the Rosecrans, Bolten, and Sanderson firm and not the most important," Kid Bradley said.

Captain Carter took another puff on his slim cigar and watched as an average height strapping man with a graying mustache pushed his way out of the crowd down the street and started toward the hotel. He wore a black broadcloth suit with a gold watch tucked into his vest pocket. He also wore a white shirt to contrast and a black bow tie. He wore a pistol to his right side tucked into a black gun belt studded with silver. He walked with a strut as if he was something to look at and he was if only for the clothes he wore.

The man walking beside him with a nearly identical mustache was as tall as Carter. Charlie Bolton or Black Bart stood a good three inches above six feet. His face was cut deeply with age lines and his eyes were cold, but the eyes were those of a man born to command. He looked like the sort of man who could be outright cold-blooded.

That meant there was still one man left for him to meet, Frank Rosecrans.

Sanderson and Charlie Bolton loomed over their table. Sanderson smiled easily, his lips hanging loosely to the lit pipe. He put out his open hand and took Carter's in return.

"It's good to see you, Carter. How was your trip out?"

"Not bad, the stage got robbed though." For this, he looked directly into the eyes of Black Bart, also known as Charlie Bolton, although it couldn't have been Charlie robbing the stage this time for he had been playing cards with Marshal Fowler at the time of the holdup.

"Word gets around fast in these parts," Charlie offered.

Letting go his hand shake, Sanderson turned to Charlie Bolton. "Charlie, I want you to meet Captain Adam Carter. If there was ever a man to ramrod this operation and carry our plans through, you're looking at him."

"What do you know about cattle?" Charlie wanted to know.

"Not a cotton picking thing," Carter admitted.

Charlie looked back to his partner and said, "I thought you said this was our man."

"He is."

"Well, he doesn't know the first thing about a cow."

Carter shifted so he could look directly into Charlie's eyes. "I know men, Mr. Bolton. For instance, in some parts, you might be mistaken for Black Bart the poet."

"You say that any louder and you'll be in a pine box before sundown, however, you've made your point." He paused, thinking. "Captain Adam Carter. Sanderson says you were under his command during the Civil War."

"I was. That was a rough time for everyone. I stayed on a bit longer fighting the Apache."

"Then you know what to expect in a fight," Charlie concluded.

"That is what you're looking for, isn't it, someone who can call the battle and win?"

Bolton was irritated. He didn't come here to be identified as Black Bart the highwayman, he had come to size up their new man. In that instant, Charlie realized Carter would do. He was the man for the job just as Sanderson insisted. He was so good in fact that he'd managed to get under his skin in no time, and that took some doing. Bolton had learned a long time ago, no one can intimidate you unless you first give them permission, but this man Carter had just done a fair job of it.

"All right Carter, the job is yours as far as I am concerned, but you still have to meet Rosecrans approval."

Just then a big heavyset man pushed into the room and made his way to where the men were meeting. "You is it?" The man surveyed every man present. "Sanderson, I've heard why you're here. I came to warn you that if you plan to take from the good hard working people of this community what they have worked hard for all of their lives, you'd better come a-shootin'. If I catch one man or any number of men on my property, I won't hesitate to send them back to you draped over a saddle."

Before either man could react Kid Bradley slipped out of his seat and turned to face the big man. "Anytime you want to shoot one of us, Mr. Bennett you can turn your dogs loose. How about right now, right here," the kid said patting his holsters with both hands.

Slowly, Carter, who was still sitting took the thong off his hammer and slid his pistol free. "Sit down Bradley. If there's going to be any shooting done, I'll do it."

Bradley never flinched. He held stock still as if he hadn't heard the captain's command. "You heard me, kid. I said sit down!"

Slowly the kid turned and looked into the eyes of Adam Carter. It was at that very moment Adam Carter knew he was marked for death at the hands of Kid Bradley. The insanity that had taken over had the kid on edge. He was about to pull his guns when Carter spoke again.

"You'll never beat an already drawn pistol, kid." Slowly Adam Carter raised his right hand above the table to reveal the pistol he held in his grasp. "Now sit down."

Kid Bradley pushed by Bennett and stormed out the door as if his boots had suddenly caught fire, stepped onto the back of a dapple gray horse and lit out of town.

Kid Bradley was a cold-blooded killer. If he had already killed or not was no matter, the fact being he was a loose cannon. Why he was on the team remained a mystery, yet Carter was more distressed than he was willing to acknowledge. All because of the presence of the man called Bennett. Bennett wore the appearance of an honest rancher, even if not the most intellectual of men. There would be honest men among the Bennett riders for the man would hire no other kind.

"Mr. Bennett, I apologize for the manner in which the kid braced you," he said slipping his gun back into the holster. "The kid is completely out of his mind today. I'll keep a close eye on him if you'll promise me one thing."

"I'm not in a habit of making promise's I can't keep, but what is it you want from me?"

"Don't let your men come to town and drink."

Bolton froze where he stood, shocked beyond measure. Bennett raised an eyebrow and stared at the new man. "What?"

"That's all. Keep your men on the ranch. If they want a drink, let them drink in the bunkhouse, just don't let them come to town," Carter said eyeing the man.

"All right, I can give you my word on that. They won't be in town for anything but business." Turning the big burly man walked away shaking his head mumbling something about, "gull darn good advice."

Bolton was distraught. "What did you do that for? You just took half of our plan and wiped it off the table."

"I came here to help you succeed. I didn't come here to goad drunken men into a gunfight which would cost them their lives. If we have to kill a man he will be sober when we do so. I don't work any other way," Carter stated plainly.

"I sure hope you know what you're doing. I'll be hanged if I know," Charlie said as he walked away shaking his head in disbelief.

"Well Carter, It's been a while. How've you been," Sanderson said pulling up a chair.

Carter looked at his old Army companion. "I've struggled here and there, but your offer intrigued me to the point I had to come."

"As it should. I have many details I cannot explain at the moment but I will enlighten you the moment I get the chance."

"That's fair enough. What's Kid Bradley got to do with all of this and why is he here? Why he ain't no more than a kid." Pausing Carter continued. "What's Bennett got to do with anything?"

Sanderson suddenly looked tired. "He's one of the squatters. He's on public land."

"And I'm supposed to move him off, is that it?"

"That's the general idea, but I called you in because I thought you could handle the job and save a few lives in the process."

"That doesn't seem to be the idea percolating in the mind of Kid Bradley."

"No, it doesn't. I didn't hire him, he's Rosecrans doing. I'm counting on you to keep a tight rein on him."

Carter smiled, almost laughed shaking his head. "That may be a full-time job."

"If anybody can do it, you can," Sanderson said.

Carter studied his old boss for a long minute. "If the land were to go to the three partners through a government grant everything is being done legally, so why all the gun handy foreigners?"

"That's what I don't know. It seems Rosecrans and Bolton have gone rogue and they are not telling anything they do. There will be nothing wrong with the government appropriation bill being moved through the house. The government has the right to dispose of land any way it deems fit. Now, if the government deeds the land to the partnership, squatters would be naturally forced to leave. That's the law as it currently stands.

83

That's why you're here. However, if there proved to be any more ranchers like Bennett, your new assignment could prove to be a very nasty endeavor."

Suddenly Carter had a bitter taste in his mouth about the whole affair. He had expected to face men such as himself, gunmen for hire, not family men who owned ranches and built upon the land. What was going on here? Someone had obviously left out a lot of important details.

Sanderson stood up and shook Carter's hand. "That's all I can tell you at the moment. It will have to be enough to get you started."

With everyone gone Adam Carter sat alone at his window table and studied the situation in his mind. He didn't like it one little bit. The entire affair reeked to high Heaven. He was going to need more information and he was going to need it fast. Whatever was going on he was a Johnny-come-lately.

The firm was trying to remove good honest citizens from homesteads that rightfully belonged to them. Right now all he could do was guess. He was going to have to talk to the ranchers and others to get a handle on things. Still, he had no authority in said matters and that would be the first thing he would need. The authority he'd come here for still waited. It was a commission as U.S. Deputy Marshal. Sanderson had said it would be provided when he arrived, why hadn't it?

Chapter 11

At the end of a long table, Gaylord Bennett stewed over his meal. He was a man who enjoyed a good steak cut fresh from the hoof yet on this night the twenty ounces of Angus struggled to get off of his plate. Recent events were nagging at his conscience. First, the boy known to everyone as Duke Robinson had successfully filed on his water rights, something he had put off for far too long not thinking anyone had the gumption to do such a thing. Now the boy was accused of murder, yet he had been shot in much the same manner as those he was accused of killing. With nine children and twenty-one ranch hands, Gaylord had become accustomed to giving orders and having them obeyed. And then there was the notice he had received to move giving him thirty days to get off of government-backed land.

"You're not eating, dear." Eunice Bennett could tell something was bothering her husband.

"Is there any sign of life from that boy?"

"He was awake for a few hours today. Why? What's wrong?"

"There's more gunmen in town. Somebody is shaping things up for a range war and the Bennett holdings are the only range around this part of the country worth fighting over. There's McCarver to the south, Sullivan twenty miles to the east and all of us are on Peace Valley range somewhere. We're the ones in the crosshairs. I need to talk to that boy."

"Eat your steak, honey. I don't want you worrying on an empty stomach," Eunice said.

At his wife's request, Bennett cut into his steak and began the elimination process by which he ate. He would eat three bites of steak, three of corn and three of beans then repeat the process until every morsel on his plate was gone.

"I know I was mad at first, but that boy has got to make it. Otherwise, we're in for the fight of our lives," he said between bites.

Eunice didn't have to ask, she knew as well as Gaylord did the boy had filed on their water. Right now, the fact Brooke seemed to like the young man was the only card her husband had to play. If Duke Robinson were part of the family, things would be settled before they ever got out of hand. After twenty-three years she was well aware of how her husband's mind worked.

"Well, Brooke seems to like him, though he hasn't said much."

Brooke's jaw dropped in astonishment. "Momma!"

Bennett looked at his eldest daughter and wondered. There was always such a possibility. Brooke returned her father's stare and laid down her fork, her eyes ablaze. "I won't be party to such a plan, I do like him, but I won't be used in such a manner. If anything happens between us it will be because we are in love and for no other reason." Pausing she looked at her mother. "Momma, may I be excused?" Eunice nodded and the girl left the room.

"Well, I guess she told us what for," Eunice spoke the length of the table to her husband.

The elder Bennett smiled. Despite the setback, he was proud of his daughter for taking such a stance. She surprised him, yet her upbringing came out in full bloom for everyone in the family to see. If nothing else, Brooke Bennett was her own woman. Deep inside Bennett was beaming, his problems temporarily wiped away by parental pride.

William Sanderson stopped along the sidewalk and pointed. "This is our office in town. To you, this is the same as headquarters, if you get my meaning."

Captain Carter took in the brick building and its surroundings. If he had an office it would be his first. "Who will I find here most days?"

"Myself, Bolton or Rosecrans. Of course, you won't, you'll be busy moving squatters off of land that doesn't belong to them."

Walking down the fifty feet of sidewalk to the building, Sanderson opened the door gently and stepped in holding the door for Carter. Once both men were inside Sanderson escorted him to an office at the far front right-hand corner. An office situated so anyone occupying it could see what was going on all over town.

Frank Rosecrans sat behind his leather topped desk and surveyed the man before him. He had papers spread out on his desk but paid them no mind. Carter was surveying things too. For instance, he had seen no less than two men in town who fit the description of Black Bart. What was going on in Peace Valley? Why didn't the town marshal recognize such men? A description of Black Bart hung on his board outside the jail though it seemed a bit smudged as if someone had erased something.

Rosecrans glanced at his partner and then back to Carter. "Sit down," he said. "You're late. I expect better from an army man." Rosecrans took a look out the window and then turned his attention back to Sanderson. "Will, this is the man you say will move those squatters off government land? This is our man?"

"Yes, sir. Captain Adam Carter of the gunboat *Essex*." His response had been in haste, a fact Carter noticed immediately, almost as if Sanderson was fearful of this man. Charlie Bolton was occupying a chair in the corner behind them where he remained silent. The three men could pass for brothers though he knew they were not. Bolton seemed remote, offering no part in the proceedings. This behavior Carter was to find out was a characteristic trait which Charlie suddenly developed any time Rosecrans was near.

"He'll do a fine job for us," Sanderson said.

Rosecrans turned his attention back to Carter. Leaning forward he nodded. "I've heard a good deal about you, captain. Your first move surprised me though." He was speaking in a most cordial manner. "To advise one of the squatters not to allow his men to drink in town, Harvey Watkins is already smarting from that one."

"Who is Harvey Watkins?"

"He owns the Divine Watering Hole. You just ran off half of his business and managed to make things a little tougher on us at the same time. My question is, are you up to the job? It seems to me you have a propensity to stack the deck in favor of the other guy."

"Anything I do will be on the up and up. I won't bait good men into a gunfight when they're drinking, and I won't do anything illegal. If you think for one moment that I will you need to pick someone else," Carter said in defense of his actions.

"Gentlemen, I believe we have our man." Rosecrans paused for effect and focused his attention back on Carter. "You'll make out swell just as long as you don't go soft. We have little time to waste. The squatters have been given their thirty-day notice and two weeks of that is gone. If they aren't moving by April first, you get them moving by whatever means necessary. Give them one more verbal warning and then you get them off. How, is your business. Move them or bury them. I'll see to it no one asks any questions, least of all me. Now, here is your commission for Deputy U.S. Marshal from Van Buren. This makes everything legal and here is your badge," Rosecrans said pulling open a drawer then tossing the star onto the desk in front of Carter. "Pin it on and get busy. You can see Wayne Thayer down at the stable for your horse and outfit."

"I do have one question before I go."

"What is it?"

"Kid Bradley, what has he to do with any of this?"

"He's your deputy, duly appointed," Rosecrans insisted.

Carter felt the air go out of his lungs as he pinned on the badge. He could have done without such help. He walked out and closed the door behind him. Then he made his way down the hallway to the front door and stepped out onto the front porch. He took in the fresh air and forced himself to breathe. He had the job, but he had never anticipated the distress he would feel once he pinned the badge on. Everything was all wrong, topsy-turvy. With uncanny recognition, Adam Carter realized he was working for the bad guys!

If he was their man, he was expendable. Carter understood that since the beginning of time, criminals had sought to gain position above suspicion or wear the uniform of law so as not to be suspected for who they really were. Thus said, he had never expected to become one of them, yet somehow he had walked headlong into a bad situation. He was in whether he wanted to be or not.

There was no way out now, not if he wanted to live. If he tried to resign now he would be killed before he could leave town. The only thing he could do was the job he had been hired for. As he stood on the front porch a young lady turned down the sidewalk in his direction.

"You must be Carter," she said as she approached him. Their eyes met and held. Once again he felt the breath leave his lungs, but this time for a different reason entirely. This time he was quite literally halted in his tracks. For a breathless instant neither of them moved or spoke, Carter felt as though his muscles were going to fail him. The girl likewise, her own eyes wide with surprise at her unexpected weakness. She faltered for a moment and then recovered. "My name is Eve Sanderson. I'm Will's niece. I hope you like Peace Valley country, I hope you like it enough to stay," she said in a most alluring voice.

"I've no doubt I'll like it here. Only death could prevent me from staying on now," Carter managed as he swept off his hat and took a bow.

Eve stared at the new marshal then at his badge in order to regain her composure.

The girl stepped past him with a wide smile and went inside. Carter stood where he was sniffing the perfume-laden breeze she'd left in her wake. Sudden as an unexpected earthquake it dawned on him, Adam and Eve. Did she know his first name? She would know. Just from the moment he had gotten to spend with her, he knew the kind of woman she was and she would not be one to overlook the details.

Finally, Carter pulled a fresh cigar from his vest pocket along with a match and lit his pleasure. He drew in the sweet aroma and started down the sidewalk. At the street, he turned toward the stables and walked past all of the businesses in town until he had reached the smith shop. There he found Wayne Thayer fitting a horseshoe.

"Rosecrans said you're holding an outfit for me."

"There's a black Arabian in the last stall. The saddle is sitting on the rail along with saddlebags, a rifle, and ammo. If you need anything else all you have to do is go down to Scranton Lane's Mercantile and sign for it. The company has an account and you're on it."

Carter studied the man for a moment. "That's mighty convenient."

"You'll find Rosecrans is a man who gets things done." The smith walked over to his anvil and hammered on the red hot shoe for a moment then dipped it in water and checked it for fit. He was a broad-shouldered man, no doubt because he used his upper body muscles all day long. He filled out much like a gorilla and didn't walk much different.

"Do you work for Rosecrans?" It was a logical question.

"I work for myself."

"I was just wondering. The last stall you said?"

"Can't miss a horse like that one," the smith said. "Been all I can do to keep him from gettin' stolen."

Carter walked down to the stall and looked in. The Arabian was just what he needed, a horse anybody could identify from five miles away. There couldn't be another horse like this one anywhere west of the Mississippi. No doubt the horse was bred back east somewhere, maybe in Kentucky, more likely upstate New York or Maryland. The pitch black coat gleamed like the feathers on a raven. If somebody didn't kill him for this horse in the first week he'd be lucky, mighty lucky.

He opened the gate and entered the stall but the horse shied from the smell of his cigar. "It's all right boy, it's all right," he said as he slowly reached for the horse's head and rubbed just above his nose. He rubbed the horse to calm him and let him get used to his smell, mostly the cigar. Then he put on a blanket and saddled the horse. He picked up the bit and bridle putting the contrivance in place with care, noting it was well out of adjustment, a sign this rig had never been on this horse. He strapped on the saddle bag and slipped the Winchester into the scabbard then he picked up the trailing reins and led the animal out of the stall.

Once out on the street, he stepped into the saddle. The horse jumped a couple of times just for fun and to let him know who was boss. Then the Arabian settled down and the two of them made their way back through town.

As he neared the office of Rosecrans, Bolton, and Sanderson, Eve was coming down the walkway so he halted the horse and waited. He removed his hat and pulled on his cigar. "Have you been long in Peace Valley?"

She looked up at the fine figure sitting upon the raven black stallion for a moment before she responded. "Not long at all, yet I've been here long enough to fall in love with this country despite what is happening to it."

"Well now, that's a mouth full," he said.

She turned a little to face the hills and pointed toward them. "I love this country, the land is so beautiful," she said lowering her hand and her eyes. "Can you understand what I mean?" It seemed as though she was searching for common ground, a fact that did not go unnoticed by Carter.

"I am a city girl captain, born and bred in Boston, but when I stepped off that stagecoach and looked out at those magnificent distant hills I knew I would never leave. The rocky mesa's far to the west, the grass-covered hills and the wild horses running there. Mr. Carter, I fell in love. This is my kind of country, and I'm going to stay right here. I'll never go back."

Surprised by her statement he studied her more intimately. He was more pleased with her statement than he could possibly confess. "You've described my feelings precisely," Carter admitted. "But what did you mean when you said, despite what was happening to it?"

"I'm referring to some of the cutthroats who are plaguing the beauty, some of the human animals who have come west to devour all that is good, to get rich and get out. Men who were bred elsewhere who feed off of the inexperience of other men less knowing. There are men who came here first who are quite brave who possess more courage and quiet dignity, but who may not understand how merciless their own kind can be."

"You speak as though you have firsthand knowledge."

"So where does that leave you, Marshal Carter? You seem to be a Johnny-come-lately."

"At your beck and call!" He paused for a moment then continued, "Any concern of yours is a concern of mine. I'm no gauge of women, but I find in you a kindred spirit for all things pertaining to right and wrong, justice if you will. I'll see the snakes head is removed just as soon as I get my bearings. And my precious lady, if you ever need to talk one on one, just send word and I'll come running. Your desires are mine."

"Then you may be removing your own head."

"Excuse me?"

"You have already met some of those snakes as you call them. In fact, you've hired on for them. I assure you at this moment I'm not convinced you're anything but another one of the very snakes you pretend to want to behead."

Stung by her statement, Carter recovered quickly. "Eve, I have instructed Gaylord Bennett not to allow any of his men a chance to come to town and drink. I'll not be a party to anything illegal or shady. If I find after riding out to meet with the squatters, I've sided with the wrong element, I shall resign and look for other work. I was unemployed when I got here and I won't do any man's dirty work."

"I don't envy your position, marshal but I shall take you at your word. At least until such a time as you prove to be one of the bad guys. Good day, Mr. Carter."

Adam Carter turned to watch the wisp of a woman walk down the street.

Eve was aware she was being watched by the marshal and walked in a tense unnatural fashion down to Scranton's mercantile then entered, stealing a glance at the man on his stallion.

Now how was he going to resign? He wasn't going to be able to, not that easily. Carter turned the Arabian and rode across the bridge that stretched across Devil's Bend.

As he cleared the bridge he put spurs to the horse and galloped away from Dead Woman Crossing, yet he could still smell the perfume of Eve Sanderson. His cigar did nothing to overcome the feeling of her presence. She would ride with him always.

Chapter 12

Adam Carter rode south on the road for a ways and then he saw where a wagon trail turned off toward the west twisting around through a couple of low hills. He was soon headed northwest toward the Bennett ranch. By late afternoon the ranch house was in sight. As he rode up to the house a young boy was sitting on the front porch swing Bennett had hung from the rafters. The kid jumped up and ran into the house as the marshal neared. Stepping down he wrapped his reins around the hitchpost and stepped up on the porch. He was met at the door by Bennett himself.

"What do you want?" The rancher was straight and to the point.

"You've been served notice. I just came out to see if you were moving."

"So, you're one of them? I figured as much."

"I'm just doing my job, Mr. Bennett."

"I own this land mister. I've been here over fifteen years and I'm not going anywhere."

"Can you prove ownership? I have it on good authority that this is government land and a bill is being moved through Congress as we speak that will grant this land to Rosecrans, Sanderson, and Bolton unless you can prove some kind of prior deed."

"Come in, Marshal Carter."

"Call me Adam."

"I only call my kids and my good friends by their first name."

Carter followed the man into the ranch house and Mrs. Bennett led them to a sitting room on the east end of the residence. Large windows offered a panoramic view of the land. The hardwood floors were made of a dark cypress and the rest of the house bespoke the work of a craftsman. Carter was envious. The Bennett family had proven up.

"Honey, would you go and get Duke's saddlebag? I believe the marshal here wants to see who rightly owns this land we call home."

Mrs. Bennett left for a moment and returned with a dark brown saddlebag. She handed it to her husband and took a seat. Though the house was full of kids, they made themselves scarce. Mr. Bennett opened the saddlebag and pulled out papers. "Here are deeds that prove the land is properly filed on and already owned. I would appreciate it if you would look them over."

Taking the documents from the man, Carter unfolded them and began to read. What he read he did not like. The land was owned by one Duke John Robinson and Ian Durant lock stock and barrel. "Who is Duke Robinson and Ian Durant?"

"Duke is our neighbor. He was shot from his horse. He's here as we speak recovering from his wound."

"Can I speak to him?"

"I'm sorry, Marshal, but he hasn't been awake much. Mostly he's still drifting in and out of consciousness," Mrs. Bennett answered.

"When he's able, will you send for me? I think he may prevent a lot of unnecessary bloodshed if I can speak with him," Carter said.

Bennett leaned forward and handed the marshal more documents. As the marshal looked through them he became weary. Every document he looked at said that Duke John Robinson and Ian Durant owned all of the water rights in the area, which meant they also owned the grazing land. It was not at all what he expected, and from the dates, the young man had only recently acquired the deeds.

"I've got to speak with that boy, just as soon as he's able."

"Certainly," Bennett said. "Have you eaten yet? If not you're welcome to stay for supper."

"Don't mind if I do. I sort of skipped a meal today."

"Well now we can't abide such trauma," Mrs. Bennett said.

Handing the papers back to Bennett the rancher put them away for safekeeping and they left the sitting room for the dining room where a meal was already on the table. Evidently, Carter caught them just as they were fixing to set up to the table. There were twelve chairs in all, and most of them full when he took a seat. The elder Bennett said the blessing over the meal and everyone started to eat.

Carter felt out of place. It had been years, he was a boy, in fact, last time he sat up to a table with a family, longer still since anyone had said the blessing over a meal. He felt embarrassed, deservedly so. His own mother would be disappointed in him if she knew how long it had been since he'd eaten food that was blessed before consumption. The food was good fare however and he soon found himself immersed in the Bennett family ritual.

If this was a squatter, Marshal Carter was an outlaw. What was it Eve told him back in town? I'm not convinced you're anything but another one of the very snakes you pretend to want to behead. These people were not a problem and he could not allow them to become one. "Mr. Bennett."

"You can call me Gaylord, and I'll return the favor."

"All right, Gaylord, if I ride out here with some men in the next few days it's only because I have no other choice and if there's to be any shooting, please remember I wear a badge. I don't care if you shoot one or ten of the scoundrels who'll be riding with me, just don't shoot me. If you do, there won't be anything I can do to stop the coming train wreck."

"That's the second time in as many days you have given me good advice. I'm beginning to think you might be on my side marshal." Bennett smiled.

"You can bank on it. Just don't say anything to the folks who got me this commission. I'm for the law and I won't stand idly by while men with no scruples interpret it and twist it to their own favor. I may have to play both sides of a coin for a time, but I assure you I'm your best friend in the matters before you. Don't do anything illegal yourself, and in the meantime, I'll try to steer their wagon in another direction."

Carter paused, then finding the words he continued. "You seem to have ownership sewn up, or at least Duke Robinson and this fellow named Ian. I was informed otherwise. Once this unexpected news is known, someone's plans will be derailed. I don't know what their reaction will be, but I can fairly guess it won't be pretty. They'll probably try to kill the boy."

"Haven't they already?"

"Someone sure did, but I have no proof it was them."

"You won't hold it against us if we shoot some varmints?"

"To the contrary, I'd be much obliged as long as I am not hit," Carter said.

Gaylord Bennett chuckled from his perch at the end of the table. "Marshal, I like your style. I'm going to like having you for a friend."

"Likewise," Carter confirmed.

Eunice looked across the table, "Marshal, we've got a spare bedroom, why don't you stay the night and ride back in the morning. I'll fix a good breakfast and you men can get to know one another better."

"I think you have me quite sold on the idea. I don't like riding about in the dark in unfamiliar territory and your cooking is the convincer."

Mrs. Bennett blushed and took another bite. The marshal was a handsome man and with more education than she was used to having around. It was going to be a pleasure to have the lawman for the evening.

When supper was through Bennett took the marshal on a tour around the ranch house and its subsequent buildings while Jackson Bennett put his fancy Arabian away in the barn. There was much to see from the cedar corral to the onsite smith shop. Carter was introduced to the men who worked on the ranch, those who were present, and he was shown the lay of the land. There were good men, the kind who would be tough as nails in any fight. They were not the type to start any trouble.

They walked around the corral and looked in at the Arabian that was nibbling a bait of oats. Bennett studied the animal. "That may be the nicest horse I ever did see."

"He's the best horse I ever saw and he's mine unless I get myself killed."

Bennett looked down at the lawman. "That might be a tricky thing considering who brought you to town."

"They know where I stand. They thought I'd just roll over and do whatever they say, and in that respect they were wrong."

"I don't figure they're going to let you live long once they discover you're your own man," Bennett said leaning on the fence rail. "But it's my pleasure to know you for as long as they allow." Pausing he added, "If you ever want a job, I've got one right here."

"I didn't like this badge from the moment I pinned it on and I like it even less now, but I'll do my job to the letter of the law. They think because they brought me here and got me a commission, they can get away with murder, but they're wrong. I won't be party to such dealings. A good honest man and his family have a right to be defended by the law. I may not always be on time, but I'll see to it justice is done. And another thing, there is a girl in town, Eve Sanderson. She doesn't like what is going on around here any more than I do. She's your friend, though she is Sanderson's secretary and his niece."

"Now that's information more to my liking," Bennett said. "I would have never guessed."

"I wouldn't have either, but I learned firsthand she's on your side."

Chapter 13

Carter surveyed his new territory as he crossed the wood plank bridge into Dead Woman Crossing. He noted a fur trapper in his fringed buckskins resting outside the mercantile and thought the man could probably recite Cicero or Aristotle. There was a young man who might have graduated Cambridge or Oxford talking to a young lady who blushed suddenly. And then there was a sun-weathered old man who looked to be a southern patriarch. All but the young lady wore guns.

That's how things stood after the war ended back east; everyone was responsible for their own safety, their own mouth, and their own doings. Freedom requires individual responsibility, he thought to himself. The only protection anyone had against tyranny was being able to wear a gun on their hip. He wore two.

Without warning, a large burly man bounded from a nearby crowd. Carter glanced his way and their eyes met. The man was obviously staggering drunk, looking for trouble. Without warning he stopped directly in Carter's path grabbing the reins of his horse forcing the Arabian to halt, certain Carter was the trouble he was looking for. Anticipating a confrontation, folks on the street halted in order to witness the proceedings.

"So!" The big man stood spread-legged facing the marshal, his shirt sleeves rolled up to reveal great massive forearms which would hold an abundance of power. "You're one of them low down land grabbers!" The man stood stock still measuring the horse and rider for a moment. "I know who you are."

Carter didn't flinch, but stepped from his saddle, took the reins from the man and led his horse to the nearest hitchrail to secure the animal. They had an audience gathering and Carter made a show of shucking his vest to reveal his U.S. Marshal badge beneath. He then laid his vest over the Arabian's neck. Carefully he unbuckled his gunbelt and hung the weapons over the saddle horn. Then he unfastened his badge and dropped it into his black leather saddlebag. Turning back to face the man he suddenly felt good. Eve was there, watching his every move, appraising him to see how he handled the unavoidable situation.

Carter's mouth was dry, yet he remained calm, his eyes focused like radiant light on the man who confronted him. He raised both hands out from his side, "As you can see I'm not going to shoot you, so let's talk. I've only been in town for a day or two, yet you seem to know more about my business than I do. How is that?" The marshal asked.

The big man had not expected to be put on the spot in such a manner. He intended to fight from the position of superiority, yet suddenly his motives were being brought into question. "I know a skunk when I see one. Them what brought you here are a bunch of sidewinders and if you work for them, you are as well."

"You're mistaken friend. I work for the people of the United States and no one else."

"Is that so?" The oversized man came a few steps nearer. "You're here to take from the good people of the territory land they have sweated and bled over. Land we have worked for years. What do you plan to do lawman? Burn us out, tear down our homes or just shoot us?"

Notwithstanding, the fact the man he faced was drunk, Carter recognized something else in the man, a brooding straightforward fear. Not fear of him or anyone else, but the fear of losing all he had. He was afraid for his family, afraid of losing his home and his ranch. He was not afraid of any mere mortal. The comprehension of that one truth touched Carter as nothing else could have and concerned him anew. More and more Carter was finding doubt with his itinerary. With each rancher he met, he grew more concerned with his choice of careers.

The gathering crowd supported the man by spouting allegations and murmurs toward the new marshal. There was no doubt as to where their sympathies lay. They felt sorry for the big man and they did not like the idea of strangers coming to town pushing everyone around. They were pitted squarely behind the big man and decidedly against the newcomer, badge or no badge.

There was a sudden faint murmur from the crowd and then an unmistakable rustling. Carter watched as the big man's face went blank staring past him to someone else entering the fray.

"Look out Dale, its Kid Bradley!" and the crowd moved back allowing more room.

The kid took a few more steps and stopped directly beside Carter. "Let me take care of this one. It's way past time this sort of sentiment was laid to rest."

"Don't move a muscle, Kid." Carter's voice cut the air like a dagger. "I'll fight my own battles. The last thing I need is you interrupting me."

"But you ain't wearing a gun!" Kid Bradley said in protest.

Dale McCarver demonstrated no desire to back down. The appearance of Kid Bradley had shaken him, but McCarver was not the same as Gaylord Bennett. McCarver was a good ten years younger, willing and ready to fight. He was going to stand his ground. He no doubt felt safe in front of so many witnesses, especially when so many of them were obviously his friends.

The big man's eyes shifted from one man to another, puzzling over what to do, so Carter took a step forward then to his left placing himself between Kid Bradley and McCarver. He was now within three feet of the big man.

"The kid has no part in this, McCarver. I've no quarrel with you, but no man calls my hand without he gets his chance. If you want what I've got, don't let the fact I'm a U.S. Marshal bother you."

Suspicion blazed forth from the big man's eyes. "You're a liar!" he yelled. "You've still got a gun!"

McCarver jerked his gun free of its holster and in the instant just before that Adam Carter moved. Carter swung his right arm connecting with McCarver's right forearm as it was coming up. He grabbed McCarver's arm with one hand then the other and as he forced the man's arm back across the hitching rail, his wrist snapped.

The gun went flying and Dale McCarver wanted out, but the marshal was not through with him. Carter stepped in and delivered a wicked uppercut to the man's jaw. While his left hand gripped his broken forearm the big man fell into the dusty street and rolled onto his side in agony.

Carter stooped, picked up the man's gun and walked over to him. McCarver was sitting up now and Carter extended his gun to him. He stood over the man letting his eyes roam over the crowd. The bigger man shook his head to remove the unexpected cobwebs and then looked up at the marshal. "You broke my arm!"

"No, I broke your wrist. I wouldn't complain, you're still alive," he added. "Take your gun and forget about it." Carter slid the revolver into the man's holster for him. He turned his back on the man and intentionally walked back to his Arabian, fully aware Kid Bradley was covering him, though it was unnecessary. The rancher was unable to draw his weapon with his wrist dangling. If Bradley interfered now, he would have to arrest his own deputy.

The marshal pushed his way past the kid then pinned his badge back into place, buckled his gunbelt around his waist and stepped into the saddle. His vest lay over the nape of his horse's neck and this is where he left it. Turning he rode toward the stable, tipping his hat as he passed Eve Sanderson in the crowd. He knew her eyes would follow him down the street so he didn't turn around. She would be pleased he hadn't killed the man. Adam Carter smiled to himself as he led the stallion into the back stall.

As he removed his saddle, Wayne Thayer appeared at the stall. "That was smooth, real professional. I never saw the like, just busted his wrist like it was a twig. There's not a man in five hundred miles that would have bet on you before today. Ninety-nine men out of a hundred would have just shot McCarver down. What you did out there was worth more than ten gunfights." Pausing, the hostler looked around to make sure no one was eavesdropping.

"You sure got Kid Bradley's attention anyway. He's been thinking he is the cock of the walk around here, nobody faster or smarter. You sure got him thinking."

"If a marshal killed every man who braced him, there wouldn't be anybody left out west within six months," Carter said as he hung his bridle.

"I never gave it much thought, but you're probably right," Thayer added then looked around one more time to make sure no one was sneaking up on their conversation. "A Texas Ranger by the name of Moe Rogers was killed right out front about a year ago. I drifted in about thirty days later, knowing the town needed a hostler and a blacksmith. Naturally, I stayed on." He checked his surroundings again, "I'm Wayne Thayer, Texas Ranger. I've been snooping around trying to find out who might have killed my friend Moe."

Carter was aware of the fact the man had taken him into his confidence simply because he was a fellow lawman. Was he aware of the risk he was taking? "Any luck?"

"Not yet, but I do know it happened during a bank robbery. Moe must have recognized somebody or everybody because they killed him on the spot. He was unarmed at the time, never had a chance, just stumbled outside at the wrong time of night best I can tell."

"So Roger's death is an unsolved murder."

"For now, but that's why I'm here. When the Rangers lose one of our own like we lost him, McNally naturally goes on the warpath, we can't stop or go home until we figure out who done it."

Carter looked at the man measuring him. "This ain't Texas."

"No sir, it isn't. I should correct myself. I'm a retired Texas Ranger."

"What about the deaths of Marty Jones and Rudy Tallmadge? Do you have anything on them?"

"No, I'm sorry I don't. Marshal Fowler seems to think it was a young kid named Duke Robinson, but I don't believe it. Tallmadge and Jones had gotten in with the wrong crowd and they knew something. I spoke with both men several times. They kept their horses right here. They were very near blabbing something whenever they got drunk, but I never was able to get them to finish talking. I think they were eliminated to keep them from talking. That Robinson kid showed up at a bad time, he's just a scapegoat."

"I see, well keep your eyes open. Black Bart is around and so is Black Jack Ketchum."

The retired Ranger shook his head and looked back at Carter. "I know, and Ben Thompson rode in this morning. He looks as meek as a baby rabbit, but he's meaner than a rattlesnake."

"That matches what I've heard," Carter said.

"Be careful, Carter. I don't have any friends around here, and there seems to be a bad element moving in. I'd sure hate to see you placed in a grave on Boot Hill."

"Me too," he said as he hung his saddle on the rail and gathered his belongings.

As Carter closed the gate behind him Thayer added, "Your horse will be ready to ride any time you need him, day or night."

"Thanks, I'll be seeing you."

Carter stopped at the barn entrance to let his eyes adjust to daylight once again. Looking up and down the street he noticed few people he could actually identify, so when Eve spoke to him from the side of the barn he was startled.

"Marshal Carter, over here," she whispered so no one else could hear.

He turned and walked to where she was standing then kept walking as the girl turned to the rear corner of the stable.

"Rosecrans is planning a raid on the Bennett ranch tonight. I overheard him and Bolton telling the kid to make sure you don't come back," she said with genuine fear in her eyes.

"I'll be. You mean I've worn out my welcome already?"

"It's nothing to poke fun at," Eve said.

Carter looked at the concern on her face. "Just how am I supposed to take news like that? There's no better way I know of."

She looked into his eyes trying to understand what he meant. "I should have stayed and listened longer, but I was frightened for you and got so excited I couldn't think of anything else. I had to warn you."

Carter took a look around at their surroundings to be certain they weren't being watched. "You did the right thing. Thanks to you, I can protect myself."

"Oh Adam, I can't believe my uncle is mixed up with these men. He would never do something like this on his own. He's a good man."

"Was he there?"

"No, I don't know where he is."

"I wouldn't go judging him just yet. Maybe he has a good reason for being mixed up with these two. Although we can't think of one, he may have one. I've worked with him before, and I just can't believe ill of him," Carter said.

"Thank you, Adam," she said and kissed him on the cheek. "I shall hold onto your words for dear life and pray you're right, that there is a good reason for what he's doing, though I can think of nothing."

He looked down into her frightened eyes. "He didn't bring me here by accident, Eve. William Sanderson knows me from the war. He knew the kind of man he was getting when he hired me and he's a man who plans every detail in a battle. I know, I was under his command for four years."

"I shall remember your words, Adam and have faith in my uncle. Thank you," she said and walked away with a quivering smile, albeit a smile.

Carter watched her walk away and every step she took betrayed the fact she was scared. She was afraid for him, afraid for her uncle and didn't know enough to be afraid for herself. She was in danger just as much as he and Sanderson were; only she didn't think one minute about her own safety. She was thinking of them. Carter shook his head and headed for his room at the hotel.

Chapter 14

At the Bennett ranch, things were happening that no one in town could possibly know. Gaylord walked around his ranch headquarters giving orders to fortify here, move something there or clear something else out of the line of fire. All the Bennett riders had been brought in from the range and line camps leaving the cattle on their own. He was preparing for a war, though he knew not when it might come.

His men knew good and well what he was up to. When they were offered a break they were cleaning their weapons and checking their loads. The old man didn't have to say what for; they just naturally knew danger was riding the wind. Every move the old man made convinced them further.

"I've never seen Bennett like this before," one of his riders said. Five of the Bennett riders sat on their bunks cleaning their weapons. "He's acting like he's seen his own ghost."

"The evidence sure is pointing in that direction," another said.

Yet a third said, "I'm not sleeping in the bunkhouse tonight, fellas. I'm sleeping out of doors in case they decide to torch the place. I was caught in a bunkhouse fire several years ago and I'm telling you, I'm lucky to be here."

"That's a good idea, might be able to surprise them if we're already in position," the first young man said.

There was some low grumbling after that, but to a man, the conclusion was to find a spot and sleep outside under the stars. No orders had been given by Bennett, but then he didn't need to give any. The type of riders he employed didn't need to have their hands held like a kid in nursery school, though mostly they were young men, orphans from the Civil War like Duke Robinson. Gaylord Bennett hired men who could make a decision and get the job done. The only standing order they had was simple; to be certain they didn't set their sights on his daughter, Brooke. So far none of the young men had tested that order, but every one of them knew about Duke John Robinson receiving the inside straight when it came to her.

In the early afternoon hours before the sun went down, thirteen men rode out of Peace Valley headed for the Bennett ranch, one of them Marshal Adam Carter. He gave his own set of orders before leaving town, orders that placed Kid Bradley riding point. There were a few snickers offered from some of the more seasoned riders, but otherwise, no one said anything.

"You're riding point, Kid. If there's to be any shooting, you'll have to open the ball," Carter said.

Bradley was just about to step into his saddle and he hunched his shoulders as if he just taken a blow to the back. The intent was obvious. If he got shot from his horse, no one was going to miss him. He'd bragged so much about how good he was with a gun until he was now riding point. If anything happened, he would be the first man shot. He stepped up into the saddle and looked at Carter measuring the man.

"I'm not about to ride point!"

"You're riding point or you aren't going with us," Carter said.

Every rider kept their distance single file behind the kid as they left Dead Woman Crossing, Marshal Carter brought up the rear. Carter knew the kid had planned to lie back if possible and get a bullet or two in his back once the shooting started. That had been his plan all along, but Carter had the advantage of being in charge. Now the crew was riding, and it would be a long ride, a time to think and plan.

Would the Bennett's be ready? Secretly, Carter was hoping the Circle B was reinforced and dug in for a fight. They would reach the ranch about midnight, not the hour an honest person would come calling, not unless he was wounded or in need of help. He knew the kind of men he was riding with, a bunch of hard cases. Not one of them knew what it was to work for an honest day's wages. They were killers for hire, gunmen who since the war's end knew no other way, men who no longer had any earthly aspirations. He had no intention getting to know any of them simply because he felt it would be harder to dispose of them when the time came. Gun handy veterans all paid for by the firm.

What was Sanderson's part in this? Was he a government official working under cover, a man taking a wild chance at riches beyond imagination, or a good man turned bad?

Eve said he was a good man and Carter agreed, so why was he involved in what appeared to be a shady land grab? Sanderson had been a good man during the war, but if Carter knew anything he knew how the war had changed many a good man. He, himself, would do nothing illegal. What about Sanderson? What was in it for him? The firm had hired him to create an appearance of respectability, but he would not do their dirty work for them. They would have to follow the law.

The closer they got to the ranch, the more the riders spread out. It was clear Kid Bradley was becoming more and more isolated. Carter smiled to himself, knowing the kid was a sitting duck in a shooting gallery. He could demand nothing of the squatters without proper backup and he knew the kind of men he rode with, the kind that might let the kid bear the full brunt of his actions, the kind of men who would be more concerned about their own skin.

As they neared the Bennett Ranch, Kid Bradley became more perturbed, aware the other men were falling back. He turned and yelled back at them. "Get up here with me you bunch of cowards."

As the men started to close the distance a voice boomed from the darkness ahead of them. "If you come any closer we're going to empty a bunch of saddles."

Every horse in the group stopped as if frozen in ice. The night was cold, about thirty-five degrees. A horse blew to clear its nostrils, and another marked time, impatiently being held in place by an experienced rider. Then a dead calm swept over the riders for they were exposed and not one of them liked what they had ridden into, a neatly prepared ambush if they pressed matters.

"You fella's turn around and go back the way you came," another voice said. "You're covered by no less than twenty one rifles, maybe more. You don't have a snow ball's chance in hell."

"You've been ordered to get off of this land," Kid Bradley challenged, his voice shaken.

"Now sonny, why would I up and leave all this land behind without taking one red cent for it when I own it lock, stock, and barrel?" It was old man Bennett speaking now.

"You don't own it, you squatted on it and the government wants you off," the kid challenged.

"Every bit of the land you're claiming belongs to the government has been filed on legally. The government can't take away land that already belongs to someone unless you become delinquent on your taxes, which we're not. If you would take the time to check with the folks back in Washington, you'd find out what I'm saying is true. You can't move me off this land. You have no say in the matter."

The kid yelled over his shoulder, "Carter, get up here and help me!"

"This is your dance, kid. I'll not impose upon these folks against their will. They seem to have filed on the land in question and if they have, there's nothing I can do but check their claim when we get back to town," Carter stated.

"We'll go back to town, for now, Mr. Bennett, but we'll be back. We'll choose a better time and we'll be back," Kid Bradley replied, his voice no longer shaking.

Turning his mount, Kid Bradley spurred his horse and rode back through the column picking up his entourage as he went. As he rode by Marshal Carter he stared at the man with contempt. The marshal fell in behind the other twelve men and set an easy cadence toward home. It had been a good night. No one on either side got shot, and a solution for Rosecrans and company seemed no closer.

Adam Carter smiled to himself. The Bennett's had been ready despite the fact there'd been no time to receive a warning from him. Gaylord Bennett was not going to roll over and play dead. He was a tactician, regardless of the fact he had never been formally educated past the fifth grade, and Carter knew how to judge men better than most.

Despite the long ride to Bennett's ranch and the fact Carter was pleased; this was not the outcome his men anticipated. They didn't come to argue, they came to fight. They came to destroy, they came to conqueror. Carter understood if he failed to move the Bennett's, it would become harder to move the other ranchers. All this talking was not in the firm's plans, certainly not in their war chest of ideas, but it was way better than a shooting or a range war no one could stop.

Pressure was building on the grassland around Dead Woman Crossing and something had to give sooner or later. Carter had been lucky on this night. He could go back and report what happened, but he would not get the kid to ride point again, and that bothered him. What would he do next time they rode together? What could he do?

Chapter 15

Duke Robinson lay awake in his room. He was thinking he liked the Bennett family and couldn't take from them what they had worked so hard to build. When they were nameless and faceless the idea had seemed easy, but now he'd gotten to know them, his plans seemed quite absurd. His plans? No, they were Ian's plans. Where was Ian anyway? Had he really gone home to take care of personal business?

There was a tap on the door and Mr. Bennett entered the room. "Well, we turned the first wave back without a shot being fired, but I doubt we'll be that lucky next time. That Carter fellow, he's a caution. I'm going to like having him around, providing he doesn't get shot."

"I've been thinking, Mr. Bennett, I was prodded into this idea of filing on your land by a fellow I don't really know, and while the idea sounded as if it couldn't miss, it seems quite foolish right about now. What once seemed easy now appears like a swindle. That's just what his plan is too, a land swindle. I would be a thief of the worst kind and I wouldn't be able to live with myself if I tried to follow through with my partner. It's your place." Duke sighed. "The problem is, I'm willing to deed your property back to you, but I don't know what Ian will do."

Silent barefoot steps had stopped in the hallway, pausing to eavesdrop on the two men.

"I'm beginning to like you, son. I have to admit, you sure got my attention as well as my daughters. I'll pay you a profit on your investment, and when you can ride, we'll

117

take a few days to help you gather them cattle back in the breaks so you'll have at least a start on your own place up at Sandstone Lake," Bennett said.

"You don't have to do all of that," Duke said.

"Oh, yes I do. You boys caught me with my pants down. I just naturally assumed because I had built my ranch here and because I ran so many cattle on so much land, I wasn't in any danger. You boys proved me wrong. You've shown me how important it is for a man to obtain the legal rights for all he does. For that I owe you."

Duke had something else on his mind, and it had nothing to do with land or rights. "Sir, I would like to court your daughter, Brooke once I'm well that is.

"That's what I like about you, son, you don't beat around the bush. I'll give my consent, as long as there's no hanky-panky." The silent footsteps retreated in the hall, yet they were quickened.

"I wouldn't think of it, sir."

"Now you are playing me. Don't forget, I was a young man once myself. You'll promise one thing and then when the two of you are alone, well you get my drift. Keep it clean and you will remain in my favor. Understand?"

"Yes sir, completely."

"I'll have to think on how to persuade your partner, you think on it too. Who is he anyway, this Ian Durant?"

"Honestly sir, I don't really know. I ran into him at Ft. Smith, Arkansas and he said all this land was ripe for settling, said all I had to do was file on the water rights and we'd be partners and build a ranch. So far I haven't seen him yet." Pausing he added. "I seem to be the only one trying to build anything."

"I see. Well, we'll keep our eyes open for the fellow. How old is he, what's he look like?"

"He's early twenty's, maybe six foot tall, sandy hair and blue piercing eyes. He's built a lot like me, well a lot like I use to be."

Bennett chucked. "Son, you'll recover. You're young. It's us older folks who have a hard time recovering from such things as bullets and sickness."

Bennett left the room and walked back down the hallway leaving Duke to himself. Things were sure a mess, and no one had any idea how they would pan out. That's the thing, you can make plans, dream and do everything just right, but someone always seemed to come along and knock you off your high horse. In Duke's life, something happened every time things started going his way.

Chapter 16

It was pushing mid-afternoon before any of the men in the raiding party began to stir. Rosecrans had been on edge all morning waiting for some kind of word about what had happened at the Bennett ranch. Now Kid Bradley was in his office filling him in on the evening's events.

"All we could do was turn back. I never got a chance at Carter. The entire evening was a bust."

Rosecrans was fuming. "So, nothing has changed!"

Eve sat at her desk and smiled. She could hear the heated argument from her own office. There was no need sneaking down the hall to eavesdrop. Adam was alive! The Bennett's held fast and the entire effort against them had failed. She was so immersed in her fantasy about what might happen next she failed to notice the abrupt silence. Suddenly the door to her office burst open and Rosecrans stood there looking almost insane, hatred burning in his eyes. "What are you smiling about?"

With such good news, she just couldn't help herself. "I'm in love, Mr. Rosecrans and I doubt very seriously you could appreciate how I feel. You, sir, have never been in love with anyone or anything, but yourself!"

"Love is it? Well quit all of that joyful noise and find out who filed on the Bennett holdings. I need the information yesterday." Turning he left her and headed back down the hallway.

"Scrooge, party pooper, I'll never invite him to one of my parties," she mumbled to herself as she began to dance around her desk, then out into the room she swayed.

Twenty minutes later, Eve Sanderson entered the land office of Dead Woman Crossing. Jim Koch sat at his desk studying over some notes concerning the government land deal and he didn't like what he was seeing. "Why hello Eve, what can I do for you today?"

"Someone has properly filed on the Bennett holdings, I've been sent to find out who that might be." She smiled.

Jim looked back at his map and shivered unexpectedly. A chill went down his spine and he looked up at the girl. "Are you telling me Bennett has suddenly filed on all his land after fifteen years?"

"Well, I don't rightly know, that's why I am here. Either he did or someone did. I'm supposed to find out who," Eve explained.

Jim looked back down at his map once again only now he had a sick feeling in his stomach. His map revealed an epic plan, a plan he'd worked on for years, and it was suddenly in peril.

"Let's go down to the station, I'll have to wire Ft. Smith for the information." Carefully he folded his map and tucked it into his vest. If Bennett or anyone else had legally filed on the home ranch, it meant his plans were in jeopardy.

No one else knew of his plans, no one but that kid from a few months ago. What was his name, Ian something or other. Jim was irritated. He'd been drinking at the time, his information had been intended for him alone, but he'd slipped up and told the kid. His plan had been so devious, he'd been afraid to say anything at all, and then that kid got him to slip up. Surely the one slip up hadn't caused the destruction of his dream.

At the station, they waited. The wire was back from Fort Smith in just under thirty minutes. The land had been filed on and the new owners were Duke John Robinson and Ian Durant.

Ian Durant! Jim Koch was beside himself. That stupid kid had outwitted him! All of his carefully laid plans now lay in ruin. The kid had beaten him to the draw. Now the question that presented itself was simple, who was Duke Robinson and where was he? The name was there, hiding in the back of his head somewhere, but where had he heard it before?

Not only had the two filed on the Bennett holdings, but they had bought all of the land surrounding Sandstone Lake. Whoever Robinson was he had moved swiftly and more decisively than Jim Koch, leaving Jim's plans drowning in despair. He had been outmaneuvered and outsmarted by a wet-behind-the-ears kid. He finally got his bearings from Scranton Lane.

Scranton Lane had not only heard of the boy as he called him, but he had sold Sandstone Lake to him.

"You mean you owned the lake all this time?"

"I did. Duke bought it just before he was arrested for murder," Scranton said.

"So, that's who Duke Robinson is, the fellow who killed Marty Jones and Rudy Tallmadge. I should have known."

Scranton Lane was not used to being interrogated. "He's accused, but let's not write the young man off just yet. What's everybody so riled up about anyway?"

"Never mind," Jim said and stormed out the door forgetting Eve had followed him in.

Scranton turned to Eve. "What's this all about?"

"There seems to be more than one or two entities trying to scoop as much free land as possible around here, there's just one problem. Someone else already owns it all." She smiled.

"Is that what everyone is so touchy about?" Scranton asked.

"Sure seems to be." Eve paused for a moment and then walked over to the counter which Scranton Lane posed behind. "Mr. Lane, who is Duke Robinson and where is he? He's not in jail."

"No, he broke out faster than Fowler arrested him. Marshal Fowler says he's out at the Bennett place recovering from a nasty gunshot wound. Doc Draper's been making his way out there pretty regular of late. He'd know more than anybody about the kid."

"Kid?" Eve asked.

"Kid, that's what I call him. He's got some growing to do if he doesn't get killed first."

Eve leaned over the counter to face Scranton. "Who shot him?"

"Nobody knows. Marshal Fowler trailed him to where the shooting took place; he was on his own land when he was shot. Made his way to the Bennett ranch and he's been there ever since. Fowler never found anything but a few old tracks. Nothing he could pin on anyone."

"So, in essence, someone tried to kill the kid who was jailed for murder. That sounds awful fishy to me," Eve said.

"Marshal Fowler thought so too. At first, he thought no one but the kid could have killed Jones and Tallmadge, but now he's looking elsewhere. Whoever shot Duke did him a huge favor. Fowler was all set to hang him, now he's looking in places he would have never looked had the young man not been shot."

"Do you think the kid is innocent?"

"I don't know one way or the other mind you, but for my money, I believe someone else killed those two men. Duke only broke out of jail to help solve the crime according to Fowler. It doesn't make sense that the young man would go to all the trouble to do everything legally, set out to build him a new place, and then turn out to be a killer. It just doesn't add up. People who build things aren't killers. They've something better to do with their hands, time, and their minds."

"Thank you, Mr. Lane. I believe the killer has to be someone else too. It's none of my business, but if you hear anything that might present a danger to Marshal Carter could you let him or me know immediately?"

"Scranton studied her for a moment. Then he remembered his first love. "I'd be happy to, miss. If I hear anything, you'll be the first to know."

"Thank you, Mr. Lane." Eve turned and walked out the door. Scranton Lane watched after her. There were good people in this town. Scranton was hoping it would be the good ones who stayed. The riff-raff was something they could do without. Turning he walked over to the corner where he kept his straw broom and swept out the store. So far it had been a slow day and the floor needed a good sweeping again.

Chapter 17

U.S. Marshal Adam Carter lay in his room rethinking the events of the previous night. He had managed to stay clear of Kid Bradley's guns if only for the time being. The Bennett land was filed on and all the other water rights in the area were owned, so there was no way the government could redistribute the land legally. Those water rights were owned lock stock and barrel by Duke John Robinson and Ian Durant. Who was Ian Durant and where was he?

Just exactly what was going on here he couldn't say, but there seemed to be many unwanted drifters in town, all men with money or looking for money.

How many were being paid by the firm? Most appeared to be guns for hire, none ever did a lick of work, yet they had money. When called on the previous night, many of them were ready and made the ride as if born to trouble. Most had fought in the war and men of that stamp had known little else in recent years, in fact, he was one of them.

How many young men from the war were still looking for a home or a place to hang their hat of an evening? Isn't that what he was doing? Until now there had been no woman with whom he wanted to share his life. Eve was different than other women, she could love him unconditionally, and she would expect great things of him. He sensed the feeling was mutual, for he knew he could expect great things from her. If he could somehow survive this crazy labyrinth of trickery and deceit he might have a chance. If not, his destiny lay on boot hill.

Getting up he shaved in his hotel room mirror then bathed with the washcloth provided by the maid. He looked at himself in the mirror for a moment when he was finished then put his shirt on. Reaching for his polished leather gun belt he strapped two Starr revolvers around his hips and settled them into place. Then he tied his holsters around his thighs and slipped into his boots.

There was a light rapping on the door. Turning, he lifted his left gun from its holster and leveled it at the door. "Come in, and if you're packing, your weapon better be holstered."

The door swung open slow and easy. A man of six feet stepped in and closed the door behind him. He was thick about the collar, but Carter recognized him almost immediately. "If it isn't my old friend, Lee Ferguson. What are you doing in these parts?"

"I'm in trouble my friend, and you're the man causing the ruckus."

"Sit down Lee, and tell me what you're referring to. I'm new here and I sure don't want my old friend upset with me."

Lee Ferguson was a hard working man who owned the slash F ranch off to the southeast about thirty miles. During the war, he had been first mate on the *Essex*. He was a cattleman now and it showed. His vest was a dark brown that matched his boots and gun belt. His shirt was blue and white check and his jeans were not blue, but a medium brown. His hat was black and he removed it and took a seat by the window where he could glance down at the street. He placed his hands on his knees and studied the marshal with wondering eyes. He dipped his head to study the floor a moment then he lifted his eyes and shook his head.

"The men who brought you in here, Rosecrans, Bolton, and Sanderson, they hired you to run us off of our land. I couldn't believe my ears when they said Adam Carter was their man so I had to come and see for myself," the rancher explained.

"Lee, I had no idea. They provided me with a commission as Deputy U.S. Marshal and brought me in, but I'm my own man, you know that. I won't do anything illegal. If they don't have the documentation to back up their play, I'm afraid they've wasted their time." Pausing he asked. "Have you filed on your land?"

"No, but I've done a great deal of work on the place. When the war was over everyone came west, picked out a spot and farmed, raised cattle, or whatever they had a mind to do. Not one of us thought about filing on land we rightfully settled on, including me. Homesteading didn't require it, but the times are changing. I know now what I must do. I just hope I'm not too late."

Adam knew about the filing by Duke Robinson, but he remained silent. If he told his friend now, he'd likely go off half-cocked and get himself or someone else killed. He studied his friend for a long moment. "You chose cattle?"

"I did. It's been a lot of hard work, and the first few years have been lean, but the wife and I are beginning to do well. Now, just when things are looking up, these men show up and tell us we have got to get off of our land." Lee was shaking by the time he finished.

"Listen to me Lee, I was hired and brought in to do just what you say, but I won't, I can't. You know me. I won't break the law. I'm a fair man and Rosecrans knows it too. We rode out to the Bennett ranch last night and Kid Bradley was supposed to kill me, but I hung back and put him on point. If I'm murdered they can blame it on the squatters and no one will be safe until they've cleaned all you out."

The word squatter cut like a knife. "I ain't no squatter, and don't call me one."

"Sorry Lee, I didn't mean it that way. They'll probably try again tonight, but I have to find a way to stop them. I wouldn't tell this to anyone but you, you're too good a man to be run off.

"Lee, there are others on the range who side with you, Eve Sanderson for one, Wayne Thayer is another. If anything were to happen to me, you make direct contact with them, they're on your side."

"Eve Sanderson? Are you kidding me? Don't you know who her uncle is?"

"That's another one. Don't underestimate William Sanderson. We served under him in the war and while he may be a son of anything you want to call him, I believe he may be working undercover in order to hang Bolton and Rosecrans, so if you have to kill anyone leave the Sanderson's out of it as a favor to me."

"That Sanderson?"

"That Sanderson."

"All right," Lee agreed, "but you had better be right. If you're not, a lot of good people could get killed."

"Listen, if you have to shoot any of the riders they send your way, shoot them all but the ones wearing a badge, even if you know them to be crooked because the moment you shoot a badge it's all over but the crying. They win."

"My my, they really did set you up, didn't they? Remember Adam, if you ride with that bunch, keep your head down. I wouldn't want to shoot an old friend, not even by accident."

"What's going on here, Lee? You know the lay of the land."

"Rosecrans seems to be pulling all the strings. It could be someone else, but he's the boss, the front man."

Lee got up and paced the room, hat in hand. "The bank was robbed a year ago and there was a fellow working at the stable, no one knew at the time he was a retired Texas Ranger. Moe Rogers was killed as the bank robbers rode out of town.

"Right after the bank was robbed, Rosecrans, Bolton, and Sanderson, showed up. Last month they told everyone they had to abandon their land and whatever was on it, handing out eviction notices. They posted their notices in the Ft. Smith paper so no one locally would see them until it was too late. About the same time, Black Bart shows up and starts robbing the stage into town. The only description anyone gives appears to match half the men in the territory.

"So you see my friend, things are bad and now enough gun hands have drifted into the area to start a one-sided range war. I say drifted, but I believe they were sent for," Lee said.

Carter shook his head. "All in the name of clearing hard working folks off their land. Why do they want all of this land?"

"No one knows. All we do know is they're swinging a wide loop and taking in nearly five hundred sections of good grazing land."

Carter smiled at his friend. "Well, that Robinson kid has upset their plans, for now anyway. They are going to find it rough going from here on, because Duke owns water rights to all the land around here, including yours."

"If he does, I might just kill him myself."

The marshal studied his friend. "Don't make that mistake, Lee. I would hate to see an old friend hung for murder."

"Well, if you have to ride anywhere with that Rosecrans bunch just remember to keep your head down. I don't want to find out when we start counting bodies that you are one of them."

"Don't worry about me, I'll be keeping my head out of sight as much as possible."

"Be seeing you, Adam."

"You take care of yourself, Lee, and do me a favor. Don't mess with Duke Robinson. Let me handle him. If you hear anything important let me know," he said shaking his friend's hand.

Lee Ferguson left the room and headed down the stairs. For appearance sake, Adam didn't move for several minutes. He now had a better understanding of what was happening, yet there still seemed to be too many strangers in town and any one of them could be a joker in the deck. One thing was certain. Dead bodies were going to start piling up if he couldn't defuse the situation.

After waiting a few minutes, he closed the door behind him and headed downstairs. He wanted to see Eve even if he couldn't speak to her. She saved his life by tipping him off and that was no small thing. When he got to the hotel lobby he glanced into the dining room and saw her eating lunch alone. He turned and went straight to her.

"May I," he asked, motioning to take a seat across from her.

"You may. What is your pleasure marshal, coffee, tea or lunch?"

"I wouldn't mind sharing lunch with you. I'm starved," he said.

"Then lunch it is." She waved the waiter to their table.

It was a strange lunch for both of them. They didn't talk about what was happening, they didn't talk about anything. The one time Adam started to say something, Eve put her forefinger to his lips and hushed him. They simply stared at one another throughout most of the meal and smiled. It was a strange cat and mouse game of affection. An experience neither of them had ever shared before. By the time their noon meal was finished both knew each other rather well, better even than if they had talked the entire time.

Leaning back Eve finally broke the ice. "You are really something, Mr. Carter."

"Can I speak now?"

She leaned over and whispered, "Might I ask a favor of you? Would you come calling this evening? I should like to spend more time with you without all of the prying eyes in town watching us."

"I would like that very much."

"Good, how about seven," she said.

Getting up from the table the marshal got up with her and pulled her chair back out of the way then walked her to the door. Lifting to her toes she kissed him on the cheek. "Until?"

"Until," he confirmed, then turned back to pay the bill. He was under a spell and he knew it, but what kind of spell it was he couldn't figure. She had him feeling things he had never felt before, thinking things he had never thought before, things he couldn't possibly explain and like a man's stomach growling when he's hungry, there wasn't a thing he could do about it.

Chapter 18

That evening the two of them were at the Sanderson home. Will and Natalie were there to help keep the conversation robust, although Will seemed withdrawn a bit willing to let his wife and niece set the tone and explore any subject they wanted while the men ate and listened. Eventually, it came time for the two couples to part ways.

Eve glanced at her aunt, then at Adam. "I'll bet it's a wonderful evening outside. Would you care to join me on the front porch, Mr. Carter?"

"It's a bit cold isn't it?"

"It won't be, not tonight," Eve insisted.

"I'd enjoy sitting with you though we haven't spoken much."

"That's a situation I'd like to rectify." Everyone stood with the two ladies while she added, "May I be excused, Aunt Nat?"

Natalie looked at her husband Will, "You most certainly may. Don't worry about a thing. Mr. Sanderson and I will clear the table."

It appeared a plan had been devised by the women to separate the men once the meal was finished and in so doing; both ladies got what they were after, a chance to spend some quality time alone with their man.

Once on the front porch swing, Adam Carter didn't know what to do with himself. Eve had two woven blankets prepared, one to lay over the swing and one to spread over them once they were settled. It was Eve who opened the conversation.

"I am so happy you're here, Adam. I so want to spend time with you."

The last bit of sunlight faded in the west and Carter didn't know how to respond to the girl. He was so afraid of saying the wrong thing he remained silent, unable to produce words that might be intelligible.

Eve took his hand in hers and he winced at her touch. Then she rested her head on his big wide shoulder and began to rub his forearm with her free hand.

"I'm going to like having you around, Adam."

The marshal's caution concerning everyone and everything suddenly evaporated into another world. He no longer felt he might be shot at any moment, he was no longer on edge and he liked what was happening. This girl soothed him and she was intelligent to boot. He could look about for many moons and never find another like her.

"Your value is greater to me than all of the women in the world combined. Your touch is worth more than all of the gold," he said.

Eve's heart began to melt. No man other than this could have made her feel so complete and now she learned he gave thought to his words before he spoke. In and of itself this was a most desirable trait. Most men couldn't come directly to the point of anything, but then neither could most women. She squeezed his arm and looked up to him kissing him on his lower jaw. It didn't matter where she kissed him she thought, she just wanted to kiss him.

They swung back and forth in silence after the kiss while listening to the dishes rattle in the house. The evening was quiet and the two of them sat holding one another's hand watching the light fade.

Eve ventured finally. "I am falling in love with you."

"I've been in love since we first met," Adam said. "Until this thing is over one way or the other we must remain as we are, two people passing in the night. If I survive what's about to happen, I'll marry you if you'll have me."

"If I'll have you? I won't have anyone but you," Eve said.

"Love sought is good, but given unsought is better," Carter recited.

"You know Shakespeare!"

"A bit here and there. Eve, I didn't want this thing called love, I ran from devotion just as Napoleon, but now that I see it's you who wants me I can no longer dodge Cupid's arrow. I should tackle the gates of Hell with a bucket of water, if only you would ask."

Taking his face in her right hand she turned her to him and kissed him full on the lips. Finally letting go she looked up into her man's eyes and said, "I am going to love life with you, Adam Carter. You just be sure and dodge any real bullets now that Cupid has my arrow in you."

Just then Will Sanderson opened the front door and stepped out onto the front porch. "I hope you two love birds can pull yourselves apart for a few minutes. I need to talk to Marshal Carter. Adam, will you join me in the parlor for a drink?"

Carter replied not figuring he could dodge the invitation. "I don't see why not."

Once in the parlor, Sanderson closed the door to the room and then poured each man a glass of brandy. The two men stood beside the burning fireplace. Handing a glass to Carter he lifted his to his lips and took a sip. "Marshal Carter, I suppose you're wondering why I'm tied in with Bolton and Rosecrans. I would like to explain."

"I've been wondering, having known you during the war."

"I assure you I'm here for reasons beyond anyone's comprehension, save yours. I'm under direct orders from the President," he stated flatly.

Carter smiled. "I knew there had to be a good reason. The Sanderson I knew wouldn't be caught in any type dirty underhanded dealings. Anything he did would be above suspicion and on the side of the law." Marshal Carter waited and sipped his brandy knowing his explanation would come.

"One year ago the bank at Dead Woman Crossing was robbed. In the bank vault was a top secret dispatch from Andrew Johnson which unveiled the government's plan to bring the railroad through town and take it right through to Santa Fe where the Atchison Topeka will meet the San Francisco. I say top secret, yet someone has developed their own plan to have in their possession all the surrounding land near the Crossing so the railroad will have to purchase right of way, at least that's my guess. I'm on special assignment to find out what is going on and make sure no one is wronged if I can."

"Now that makes more sense than anything I've heard since I arrived."

"I don't think Rosecrans or Bolton knows anything about the dispatch or that the railroad is coming through here. I haven't found any evidence pointing to any knowledge of it. I think they're just land greedy men who see a way to turn a profit and then get out. I'm coming up empty, yet someone is making a move. Duke Robinson has filed on all the land anywhere near here. He has a partner named Ian Durant. They were no doubt in on the bank robbery." Unfolding his wallet Will held out his Secret Service badge for Carter to see. "We've counterfeiters too. The president wants them stopped before they destroy faith in our currency."

Adam Carter sat down stunned. "I suppose you're telling me this for a reason."

"I'm coming up empty. I need your help. I can't believe that a runny nose kid could cook up a land swindle and make himself rich overnight, not by accident. He has help from somewhere."

"Johnson hasn't been in office very long," Carter said.

"Yes, but the president understands if the counterfeiters go unchecked, the United States currency system will implode on itself and a hundred dollars won't be worth a solitary dime. It will cause rampant inflation and the Federal government will have been defeated, not because of war but by what came after.

"If we can't round up the counterfeiters the Federal Government is doomed. All the sacrifice we've made to preserve the Union and remain the United States of America will be for naught," Sanderson said.

"And I thought I had a lot on my plate."

"Now you know why I brought you out here. Everything I've told you must be kept in strict confidence.

Not even my wife knows what I'm investigating. In fact, she doesn't even know I'm a member of the Secret Service and have been since Lincoln commissioned us to go after the counterfeiters the day he was shot."

"You're telling me Lincoln signed the order creating the Secret Service on April 14th 1865?"

"Exactly, he died the following morning."

"You certainly know how to make life interesting, Will."

"More brandy?"

Marshal Carter held up his glass to be refilled. Carter took a sip from his glass. "It is possible that Bolton and Rosecrans were in on the robbery last year and got the inside track on what was about to happen."

"I've thought of that, and it makes sense, but I don't have proof nor have I found anything to support that theory."

"You need proof?" Carter asked.

"We can do nothing without it. My hands are tied. I'm working on the inside, but I haven't come up with anything but suspicion."

"I see. Then I'd better help you find some kind of proof."

Changing the subject they talked of lighter things like love, death, and Shakespeare. Once they were laughing they couldn't hold the ladies at bay any longer and the quartette spent the evening laughing, playing games of knowledge, and getting to know one another. The evening lasted far into the night until the lamp at the Sanderson residence was the only lamp in town still lit.

One set of eyes focused beneath furrowed brow watching the home of Will Sanderson from a distance. A madness was slowly coming full boil, a pure hatred for one Adam Carter, along with a splash of jealousy thrown in. "So, she's in love is she?"

Chapter 19

The Bennett Ranch was not willing to let anyone surprise them. Though it was cold, men slept outside in case of a night raid and guards were posted. Inside the house all was quiet but for Duke Robinson's room. He had spent most of his day awake for the first time in a long time. He felt better and the family had been getting to know him, spending precious time with him earlier in the evening. Now, however, the family had gone to bed.

Small footsteps from a barefoot stalker made their way down the hall in silence. At her door, Brooke Bennett held up and waited to make sure there was no other sound in the house. She couldn't hear her father snoring down the hall as usual, and that worried her. Otherwise, there was no sound. With deft fingers, she reached down and turned the knob that opened the door to her room. She knew there would be a slight squeak, and she knew just when to slow down the door's movement to avoid it. Once in the room she eased the door back into place and closed it tight.

Since Duke had shown up on their doorstep she'd taken leave from her job in town and had stayed home to help her mother and Doc Draper do all they could to save him. Now he was getting along better, she wanted to talk.

Duke was almost asleep when he heard the creaking of the door as it swung open. He watched as Brooke entered the room and sat beside him on her own bed.

"If your father finds you in here we're both going to be in trouble."

"If I was going to get in trouble, it would have already happened," she explained. She slipped her hand into his and squeezed it. "I hope you're not afraid of me, Duke. I shan't hurt you. I only want to hold you for a little while."

Duke's first reaction was fright, but then he had the idea she had been in his room before, sometime in recent past while he knew nothing of her presence. She was pretty and she smelled wonderful, yet what she had in mind on this evening he knew not. She slipped into bed beside him and holding his hand, kept her figure above the quilt. Her face was so incredibly close to his he could feel her breath on his neck.

"Who are you, Duke Robinson? Why are you here?"

At least she still wanted to talk, he thought. "I'm just a young man who wants his own place. I bought Sandstone Lake. I just have to stay alive long enough to keep it, despite the fact somebody wants me dead."

"That's not what I mean. Who are your parents, where did you come from?"

"My parents? They both died. I grew up on the streets of St. Louis fighting for whatever I could get. I rode with Captain Bowlin for a time. I've not had a home for the last four or five years, not since the war started back east. Everyone who came to St. Louis since the end of the war seem to be going west, so I decided the future was west and I might as well join them. Here I am."

"But you came buying property, and with money. You planned, didn't you?" Brooke rubbed his arm as she whispered.

"A lot of good it did me. I got shot right off and I'm accused of a double murder to boot. If I live to the end of the year I'll be surprised."

"But you didn't kill anyone, did you?"

"I would never kill anyone," Duke said, then he remembered killing his own brother. "But in self-defense. If I go to trial with the evidence Marshal Fowler has against me I'll hang for those killings and the real killer will get off free as a bird."

He couldn't overcome the feeling of her breath on his neck. He never wanted her to leave his side, but he knew she would have to. Either that or there was going to be a shotgun wedding and he was going to be the unwilling groom, not that Brooke wouldn't make a wonderful wife it was just the idea of having to do such a thing with a shotgun on you. When Duke got married he wanted the event to be on the up and up, pure as the wind-driven snow and his wife needed to feel the same. There were no wedding bells in his plans, not yet anyway. He had a ranch to build and he wanted to be a notable rancher before he ever asked for her hand in marriage.

"There must be some way to prove you are innocent," she whispered.

"If there is, it wouldn't do any good. Once everybody knows I've filed on their land, I'm as good as dead. I'll never be able to get my house built before next winter, not now."

"The house can wait till next spring and you can stay right here if you have to, but we need to figure out how to prove you're innocent," Brooke repeated.

"I don't know. There has to be some way."

"First off, you have to slow down. You're starting to get well enough Marshal Fowler is going to throw you back in jail real soon. You can't do anything if you're behind bars. You have to remain ill for a long time, bedridden. Then maybe I can do some snooping around in town and learn a few things. As a waitress, I picked up all kinds of information just from overhearing conversations. It could work. But I'll have to return to my old job during the day."

"You would do that for me?"

"I would. I know you aren't a killer. And if we're lucky maybe we can find out who really killed those men," she said.

"Okay, I'll be really sick tomorrow when Doc Draper comes to visit."

Brooke kissed him then, long and hard. When she finally stopped she said, "I wish I could stay here with you, but you know I can't." Then she got up and kissed him one more time just as before, but this time she stopped a little sooner. "I don't know why I believe in you, Duke Robinson, but I do." With that, she tiptoed out of the room and back down the hallway to where she was the guest of her younger sister.

When she got into bed Lisa asked her quietly, "Well, is he feeling any better?"

"You little possum, you weren't asleep at all," Brooke accused.

"I wonder just what secrets you're keeping," the younger Bennett asked.

"Nothing you'll ever find out about. Now go to sleep!" Brooke said.

Chapter 20

Rosecrans, knowing he could not get Carter to subvert the law decided to send the kid in his place. He needed a job done under the cover of darkness and he needed it done right away so he had enlisted Kid Bradley to lead the charge, this time while Adam Carter was sound asleep in his hotel room. Nine minutes after Brooke returned to her bed the first shot was fired and for the next five minutes, there was no let up in the action. Grabbing her sisters, Brook took them to her room for cover. Three of the younger boys soon found their way down the hall to where their sisters were in the darkened room and Eunice Bennett settled in with them away from the windows.

It was a siege that did not bode well for the attackers. The first shot fired lifted Wolf Hayden from his saddle for the last time. Hayden had been riding point and never had a chance. The men had ridden into an ambush, yet several of the attackers were suspecting nothing less and dove for cover at the first sign of gunfire. Fifteen men had come to raid the Bennett ranch, but now they were pinned down at the edge of the road near the trees. Several had been wounded but not bad.

Bradley called into the night, "If they're in the trees, make for your horses and we'll raid the ranch anyway. All of their guns are out here," he yelled.

Scrambling for their horses the men were allowed to get into their saddles and made their way closer to the ranch. They gathered out on the plains to the south away from any tree line and once Kid Bradley had a count they headed in. Eleven men were along for the second attack, but Bradley had made a critical mistake. He believed Bennett had placed most, if not all, his riders in the treeline along the road to the ranch. He was mistaken and his mistake cost him dearly.

As the riders neared the ranch house guns blossomed flame, saddles were emptied and men dove for cover. In less than thirty seconds, no rider remained on horseback. Of the eleven who rode into the yard one would never get up again and several were wounded, including Kid Bradley. Back at the treeline three of the four men were still breathing, Jim Slater, Rodney Hamlin, and Ian Durant. Slater would never be the same.

Gathering up the wounded men, Jack Bennett led his victorious riders back to the house to see how things had turned out for his father's crew. He rode with caution knowing full well things may not have gone as well at the ranch. He had ten riders with him and Gaylord had kept the remainder on site scattered about in strategic locations prepared to defend the Bennett holdings to the death. Of all the Bennett riders only one was injured. Cole Zimmerman had a slight shoulder wound, but nothing life-threatening.

When Jack rode into the yard with his men it was obvious the cleanup was underway on the home place already. He slid down off his horse and walked over to his father.

"That kid Duke is one smart fellow. I didn't like him none at first, but he's turning out to be intelligent."

"You're referring to his plan," Gaylord asked.

"You betcha, Pa they did just exactly like he said they would and we were ready because he knew what they would do."

The elder Bennett looked at his son. "I never heard of Nathaniel Bowlin the Swamp Fox until we met Duke. Right now, I'm glad the boy rode with him for two years during the Civil War."

"Me too, Pa."

"Jack, let's give these fellows an escort back to town. Make sure none of them have a holdout, take five or six good men with you and try to be home by breakfast. We'll bring in the dead tomorrow."

Two of the Bennett men helped Kid Bradley into his saddle and then Jack led thirteen disarmed survivors away followed by six of his own men.

When Gaylord Bennett finally entered the house his wife Eunice was there to greet him. "Well, how did it go?"

"We didn't lose a man." He paused for a moment not sure if he was bragging or just stating fact. "They're pretty shot up."

"And Marshal Carter?"

"He wasn't among them. Kid Bradley tried this on his own. There was no sign of our friend."

"Thank the Lord in Heaven above. What about the kid, is he all right?"

"Jack is taking him and the others back to town as we speak. His pride may be hurt, but that's all. He'll be hurting for a while though."

Eunice threw her arms around her husband and gave him a big hug. "So everything Duke said was true."

"It sure looks that way," Bennett said as he looked down into the eyes of his wife

"Come on, let's go to bed. I'll be getting up early in the morning."

It took a good hour to relate the evening's events to Duke, who never moved from his bed. The entire family, but for Jack, was in the room with him. Several times later that evening it seemed like the entire ranch was in his room, and it wasn't long before he began to get weak from all of the excitement.

There was no other way to say it, but the boy had known exactly what the men who worked for the firm would do. He seemed to understand them like no one else. He had suggested the defense for the ranch and the Bennett riders had perfectly executed his plan.

Chapter 21

The following morning at breakfast, Duke Robinson joined the family at the table for the first time. He'd heard the news the night before and was more than a little surprised. Duke didn't consider himself a great thinker or tactician, he only knew what he would do and based on that he suggested to the Bennett's a plan of defense. Duke believed the fact his plan had worked so perfectly was pure luck.

He took his seat at the table that morning humbled by how he was being treated by the family he'd intended to displace. Everyone was present including Jack who had just gotten in from town. Once the food was blessed Duke ate in silence wondering what would happen next.

"How are those fellows, Jack?' Bennett asked, wanting to know about the men Jack had escorted back to town.

"Kid Bradley is all right, I think we hurt his pride more than anything. Rodney Hamlin will make it too, but Wolf Hayden may not. We left him with Doc Draper. He said if we were worried to check back with him in a couple of days," Jack told his father.

Bennett studied Duke from the end of the table and then said, "Duke, what are your plans?"

"I don't know. I'll have to turn myself over to Marshal Fowler right soon it appears."

"With such a shortage of honest men in these parts, I think I can get the marshal to let me keep an eye on you. There isn't any chance of you running is there?"

Duke looked at Bennett with a puzzled face. "Heck no, I want to find out who killed those men."

"Good boy, I was hoping you would say that. You stay here and rest a while. I'll see the marshal and try to work something out. He's been looking elsewhere since you were shot anyway." Bennett looked around the table at his family. "You say someone brought you to the house that night?"

"Yes, sir, an old man with dark green boots. I never saw his face clearly, but his boots were very unusual. They were just like the ones Scranton Lane has at his store," Duke said while remembering other strange things he was afraid to mention.

"Marshal said the only tracks he could find were yours and the man who shot you. The shooter's tracks played out back in the breaks off to the west."

"There had to be other tracks," Duke protested. "I know someone brought me here."

"Well, if you say someone brought you here, we believe you, but yours were the only tracks he found, because I looked too."

Duke thought back to that night when he was delirious and remembered the cowboy appeared to have wings of some sort on his back. He shook his head to get rid of the vision. Angels might exist, but he had no truck with them. He'd never seen or heard tell of one. Anyway, why would an angel bother to help him? Then again, who was to say it was a good angel? Wasn't Satan a fallen angel? "Maybe I was seeing things. I was awful bad off that night."

"Well, in the condition we found you, you're lucky to be alive."

"Mr. Bennett, I'll sign your land back to you, but I don't know what Ian might do. He's the joker in the deck."

Jack intervened. "Pa, one of the men we escorted back to town last night was Ian Durant."

"Duke lowered his fork and looked over at Jack. "So, you mean to tell me Ian was riding with that bunch?"

"He was," Jack stated.

"I'm going to hunt him down just as soon as I'm well enough."

"Let's not worry about him just now. The fact is he can't do anything without you. In the meantime, we've got to get things in shape around here for better defense."

"I'll just sort of hang around here and see if I can get on a horse again, but I won't go anywhere, not yet."

"You're in no condition to make a long hard ride yet. Save yourself for that spring roundup. There will be plenty of bone-jarring work then."

Bennett, Jack, and Brooke headed for town right after breakfast and Vance saddled up the dun for Duke. Vance was eighteen years old and the second oldest boy next to Jack. He was two inches taller and broad in the shoulders. He was already battle tested and country tough when it came to skinning coyote's, both two and four-legged ones. He let Duke have the lead. First, they tried to backtrack Duke's horse for a way, but they soon realized too much time had elapsed since that night and there simply were not enough tracks to study.

Giving up on the idea of finding the man in the green boots, Duke asked to see the ranch which was once his. "We'll want to stay close. I just don't know how much I can do yet."

"I'll be glad to show you some of the more interesting sights," Vance said. "I'll go easy on you."

The two were no more than a mile west of the main house when they turned north. At times the boys could see the house in between the rolling hills yet they kept riding. Soon they came to a buffalo wallow that had now been adopted by cattle. The wallow was fifty yards wide and seventy yards long full of mud and bones. "Take a look out into the middle and you'll see bones of an animal we can't peg. None of us know what it is. You have any idea?" Vance prodded.

The boys rode on and eventually came to the old Sagebrush mine. It was boarded up, but as the two rode up to the entrance, it was obvious someone had been here, peeled the boards off and went inside. Stepping down from their mounts the two young men made their way past the entrance and took a look into the mine.

"What is that?" Duke asked.

"I'm not real sure, let's take a closer look."

The two stepped closer to get a good look and then Duke looked at Vance. "That's a printing press."

"What would a printing press be doing in an old abandoned mine?"

Turning Duke made his way back toward the entrance and stooped down to pick something up. It was a spent cartridge from a .45. Duke tossed it in his hand for a moment and looked out over the terrain. "This is the casing from the shell that I was shot with. I was shot right out there on the flat."

"Let me see that," Vance said.

Reluctantly Duke handed the shell casing over. He wanted to keep it as a souvenir. "It's not every day a boy finds the shell from the very rifle he was shot with."

"No, I guess not. You know what that printing press is doing in here?"

"I don't have the faintest idea," Duke said.

"Someone is printing counterfeit money," Vance suggested.

Vance looked at the shell casing more carefully, tilting it from side to side. "We'd better get out of here and get back to the house. You were shot because you got too close to someone's counterfeiting operation."

"You think that's why?"

"I'd lay money on it. Come on, let's go before that same someone catches us here."

Vance handed the shell casing back to Duke and the two mounted up. What they found was a mystery, yet it explained a lot of things, only they found nothing that would tell them who was behind such an operation.

The boys picked their way back to the ranch house slow and easy, taking the time necessary to watch their back trail. When they ambled into the yard the stable boy walked out to meet them and took their horses, leaving the two young men free to head for the house.

Vance burst through the front door and Eunice met the boys coming in. "What in blazes is going on with you two," she said halting them in their tracks.

"Mama, we know why Duke was shot. Tell her Duke!"

She turned her attention to Duke and waited.

"Well ma'am, I was shot because I got too close to someone's counterfeiting operation."

"How do you know that?"

"We just found the printing press up at the Sagebrush Mine, that's only a few hundred yards from where I was shot. We even found the shell casing from the rifle that shot me," Duke said as he pulled the casing from his pocket and showed it to her.

"I'm giving you boy's strict orders to stay away from that mine. I don't want either of you shot. Whoever is behind this is likely the same person who killed Rudy Talmadge and his friend, Marty. Now go and wash up for lunch.

"Lisa, you and Amber come to the kitchen with me and help me get something started. You boys tell the crew to be on the lookout for anything strange. If what you say is true, we need to stay on alert." Eunice gathered her skirts and headed for the kitchen.

"Vance, can you select a couple of good men who can ride to meet your father on his way home? It would be very lousy timing were something to happen to him or anyone else."

"I'll get Duce to rope a couple of fresh horses and I'll have men in the saddle before you know it," Vance said.

The two young men walked out on the front porch and gathered the men who were in shouting distance.

"Gentlemen, listen up. Dale, you and Wiley ride out to meet dad, he's made town with Brooke and Jack by now. See to it they get home safe. Don't mess around, bring them home quick as you can and be careful. Remember, Duke was shot just a little ways from here."

Dale and Wiley mounted up. They checked their guns and ammo then turned their horses from the coral toward town. Once they were well on their way the rest of the men took up positions around the property understanding the situation as they did. Duke and Vance sat on the front porch talking as they waited for the remainder of the family to return.

"Well, no matter what happens now, you're the rightful owners. I need to speak with that U.S. Marshal," Duke said.

"Pa's pretty good at knowing what to do."

Just then the rest of the Bennett boys came out onto the front porch to wait for their pa. Dudley was fifteen, Jason fourteen and Gibson nine while Howard was only six. The two girls Lisa and Amber were busy helping their mother prepare something to eat.

"This is crazy Duke, who would try a counterfeit operation in the middle of nowhere?"

"I don't have a lick of proof, but I can make a pretty good guess. Ian Durant. Besides, if I'm out of the picture all the land rights belong to him."

Vance whistled. "Oowee. Isn't he your partner?"

"He's my partner all right, but I'm about to change all of that. I couldn't have been any dumber. I didn't even know him," Duke said.

Chapter 22

All was quiet when Carter stepped inside the Devine Watering hole. He was tired, and he wanted to rest, but first, he wanted to talk with Harvey. The room was dimly lit and Harvey was polishing glasses behind the bar. He glanced up and sat a glass and a fresh bottle of whiskey on the bar. Carter had never cared much for whiskey, but it cut the dust from his throat and gave him a chance to prepare his words.

Carter started the conversation. "Have you lived here long?"

"Why should I talk to you? You've run off half my business."

"I'm sorry about that old timer, but it had to be done. Your business will be restored, sooner than you know. Now, how about an answer?"

"I'm coming up on fifteen years later this summer. I was here long before last year's bank robbery. Things were mighty good before that, mighty good in the old days. No trouble from the local Indian's, and no outlaws to speak of, but the end of the War Between the States changed all that."

"It's going to change some more, Harvey. I'm guessing things are going to change a lot. For the better, I hope."

"There is surely room for change, and believe me, I'm ready to see some."

"Where do you stand with what's going on?"

Harvey sat down the glass he'd been polishing, turned and put both hands on the bar. He looked Carter right in the eye. "Not in the middle, and I don't stand with any of the ranchers either. As for you, I'm not for you and I ain't against you in any fashion."

Carter stared at him. "You don't sound like much help."

"No help at all. I have a well-oiled enterprise here in Dead Woman Crossing, as long as certain folks don't go telling every rancher in the country not to come to town and drink. I keep my nose out of other folks business and in return, I keep my hair. I was here before any of the ranchers except Bennett. He's been around a long time."

"Sorry about that order, my friend, but I had to do it. I plan to settle here myself. I don't know if everything will work out where I can, but that's my intention. I plan to be here long after many others are gone.I'll find some way to make it up to you."

"You sure picked a dangerous job for stayin' among the living."

"I know what I'm doing."

"Never said you didn't, but you fight shy of Rosecrans and Bolton. Some in that crowd just ain't human. They have no scruples. They'd slit your throat the minute they don't figure they need you anymore." Harvey paused for a moment. "I've seen you with Eve, she's Sanderson's niece and that makes her off-limits."

"Maybe, but not for me."

"What makes you so special?"

"You'll have to ask Eve."

Harvey studied the young man across from him. "As for the local ranchers, they're all right, just not sure where things are headed at this particular moment. I think they're all a bit scared."

"I've picked up on that. As long as I'm around, they're safe."

Harvey turned back to polishing his freshly washed glasses. "You sure enough set store by yourself, mister."

"No, I just know what I'm capable of."

"So do I," Harvey smiled and kept polishing glass.

Carter left the building and untied his horse. He walked the animal over to the stable where Wayne Thayer was shoeing a mule. Then he guided his Arabian to the back stall. Still, he didn't have a name for the horse. Just then it hit him, "All right, I think I'll just call you Lancelot. Get some rest while you can, because I got the feeling you are about to get plenty of exercise."

Slowly Carter loosened the saddle. He eyed the horse head to tail while doing so. "I sure hope I don't get myself killed riding you. Sure as I'm standing here some fool cowboy is going to try and steal you away. I just hope and pray that doesn't happen, for your sake and mine."

Pulling the saddle clear, he placed it over the railing. Then he pulled the blanket and laid it out to dry. Picking up a brush he began to brush the animal and contemplate what was going on.

Everyone in the territory was walking around on edge. Not just the Rosecrans and Bolton firm, but all the ranchers, along with everyone in town. Carter could feel the lid about to blow off. He had no idea when or how, but something could happen any moment. His thought was a simple one. Trouble never offers up an odor in advance of its arrival, but leaves all kinds of stench once it has arrived. Shaking the thought from his head he unhooked Lancelot's bridle and hung it by the door.

Back in his room, Carter had some real time to think. Harvey as much as said Eve was off limits, but he didn't believe it. He knew her better than that. Harvey could believe whatever he wanted. The man had his own ideas and his own way of thinking. Maybe, the way he felt about Eve was the one thing that would do him in. He had to be careful to keep his distance from her until things settled down. He could only hope that Eve would understand. The last thing he wanted was to place her in harm's way.

He knew his own strength and weakness. He knew or suspected what was happening. He matched up well against other men, and he knew he'd be called on to use that strength, but for now, there was no real demand, and while he didn't want to wait, there was nothing else to do.

If Rosecrans and Bolton were to make a move, it would likely happen during spring roundup. They would engineer some sort of fight between the ranchers. If half the ranchers were killed in a gunfight, Rosecrans and Bolton could move right in and take over.

He had just returned from a ride to investigate what was going on outside of town. There he was warned away by an Indian girl on a horse. She'd indicated there were men up ahead just waiting to ambush him. Were those men working for Rosecrans and Bolton? The Indian girl didn't know who they were but said their intent was obvious.

The mine, of course, he was getting too close to Sagebrush Mine. He had ridden the long way around to see if it was really there. It was located on the back side of

Sandstone Lake. Not only was the mine there, it held a printing press and evidence of being recently used.

Just then there was a knock on the door. "Carter, open up!"

He opened the door immediately for two reasons. He knew the voice, and he knew by the man's tone something was wrong.

Sanderson stepped into the room with a look of horror on his face. "They've taken Eve. They told me if I didn't go through with their plan they would kill her."

"Who took her?"

"Rosecrans and Bolton, they said she'd be safe as long as I did what I was told."

"And what is that?"

Sanderson held out a piece of paper. "There are six men designated to shoot up the Stockman Association's meeting in the morning. I have a list of ranchers who are supposed to die."

"I didn't think they would try anything like this."

"Rosecrans is out of his mind. I thought he was going to shoot me on his way out the door with Eve."

"Where do you think they've taken her?"

"They have to be heading for Sandstone Lake. Sagebrush mine is out there somewhere."

Carter took the list and unfolded it. Reading he could see it was dead on just what he expected, only he'd been thinking spring roundup. Every rancher was to be eliminated in a hail of gunfire. He folded the piece of paper and placed it in his shirt pocket then he picked up his gun belt and strapped it on.

"They're on to you, Will."

"Yes, but I can't figure out how they found out."

"I've about eight hours to find her and set her free, and you think they headed for the Sagebrush Mine?"

"She means everything to us, Carter, please find her."

"She means everything to me too. I'll find her."

Carter didn't wait for an answer, stepping through the doorway into the hall and down the stairs. He crossed the ground to the stables with urgency. He saddled up Lancelot and rode out. He was going to get her back or die trying.

It was now full dark and he had a lot of ground to cover. Not only that, he was getting mad. The idea that anyone would kidnap an innocent young lady had him fuming. The idea it was Eve had him almost out of his mind.

The worried look in Sanderson's eyes had been enough to warn him things had gone awry, but how bad were they? He knew Rosecrans was diabolical, an evil man with evil in his heart. Most of the time it lay dormant, but now his dogs had been unleashed.

He knew exactly where the mine was located. All he had to do was get there and with any luck take Eve back from Rosecrans and Bolton. If they hurt her in any way, he was prepared to extract his own kind of justice. Not anything you might find in a law book, but swift and to the point.

Riding swiftly he came to the bottom of a low valley, jumped a small creek and kept riding. The grass was tall and dry, though it was coming onto an early spring. The higher elevations didn't offer such tall grass. He set the Arabian to a steady distance eating gait and held on. "Lancelot, if they hurt her in any way this is going to get reeeeal ugly."

Crossing the valley floor he swung around what locals were beginning to call Cowboy Junction and turned north. It was a good ten miles, but he wasn't stopping or slowing down until he reached the mine. If they were not holding Eve there he had no idea where else to look. It was a longshot, but he had nothing else to go on.

He skirted Sandstone Lake and topped out on the rise overlooking Sagebrush Mine. There were no lights visible. He saw no movement, but from this distance in the dark of night, he did not expect to, especially if they were holding his girl down there. No horses were visible, so it was possible they were not present. He stepped down from his horse and staked it to the ground, shoving the stake in with his boot so as not to make a sound.

Slowly he made his way over to the mine, listening for any sound, any movement that might offer itself. There was none. As he neared the entrance, he thought he heard a faint noise coming from inside. He eased himself off to one side and sat down to ponder what it was he'd heard. Then, with no warning, the noise resumed. It was a light scratching sound.

Then he heard a grunt and knew instantly who was inside. "Is that you, Eve?"

"Adam, look out, it's a trap."

Adam Carter turned immediately to see Rosecrans and Bolton bearing down on him. Both had their guns out and were about twenty yards away. He didn't wait for either one of them to shoot. He palmed his revolvers so quickly both men were startled and missed with their first shot. Carter didn't. Both men went down in a hail of gunfire. As if on signal, it began to rain. Carter looked at the unmoving silhouettes.

The Deputy U.S. Marshal immediately turned his attention to Eve. He stepped into the mine where he heard the voice and almost tripped over her. With the rain, darkness seeped into every corner of the mine. With his brute strength, he lifted her over his shoulder and carried her out to the small cave entrance. Sitting her on the edge he stepped behind her and untied her hands. Then he untied her feet.

"Rosecrans lost his mind! He planned to kill every rancher in the area along with you."

"I know. I have the list in my pocket of the people he wanted dead. I got it from your uncle, but I didn't see my name on it."

"He had you marked special, trust me, but then," her words trailed off.

He stood her up and took her in his arms. "Are you hurt?"

"No," she said, searching his eyes. "Adam, we have to get back to town. We can't just let those men die."

"Come on."

One of the men on the ground moaned and Carter stepped over to where he was. It was Charlie Bolton.

"I need help," he managed.

"I'll send doc out for you."

"That'll take hours," he was forcing his words.

"Well, you and Rosecrans have left us no choice, you're just going to have to wait on Doc."

Bolton had slung his pistol wide when shot, so Carter paid him no mind. It was a pretty fair walk back up the hill to where he had left the Arabian, but the horse wasn't going anywhere with such good grass to eat. He pulled the stake and dropped it into his saddlebag then stepped into leather. He pulled Eve up behind him and headed back toward Dead Woman Crossing. It was a cold and wet ride.

He fairly wore Lancelot out getting to Sagebrush Mine, and now he was returning to town, some thirty miles away riding double.

There was no doubt what would happen in the morning. The meeting would begin in just a few hours. Every rancher in the area would be headed for Dead Woman Crossing and a showdown being forced by men with evil intentions.

As sunlight overtook the darkness, it was clear enough to see the rain was moving off to the east, but everything was wet. Carter led his horse down the long hill into town. He crossed the bridge and rode directly to the Sanderson residence. Helping Eve down, he led her to the front door.

"You stay here no matter what. I don't want to be worried about you with everything I have to do this morning. While you are at it, say a prayer for me. I'm going to need it."

"Be careful Adam, *I* need you."

"I'll be careful, you just make sure you keep your uncle at home. Don't any of you come out until I give the all clear, understand?"

"Yes, Adam." Eve leaned forward and kissed him lightly on the cheek.

He looked her in the eyes and took a step back. "You do as I say, I don't want you, or anyone else in this home to get hurt. The best way to ensure that is for you to stay inside, you got that?"

"I understand."

"Good, make sure your aunt and uncle don't go anywhere. I can't afford to worry about what's happening here when my attention needs to be on that meeting."

Just then the front door swung open and Adam took the initiative to kiss Eve on the cheek as she turned her head to one side. Turning he took up his reins and started down the row of buildings to the stable. At the stable entrance was Wayne Thayer.

"You've been riding hard."

"Had to, can you put my horse up for me? I have to talk to someone."

"You can do that right here," Thayer said taking the reins. "Rosecrans is fit to be tied. You're making a powerful enemy out of that man," he said as he led the horse back to its stall.

"All I had to do was show up for that. Anyway, he's dead. He thought he was buying a slave. He was a little surprised to find out I have my own way of handling things."

Wayne Thayer stopped in his tracks halting the Arabian. "Well, he was might bothered with your shenanigans. You say he's dead?"

"He and Bolton tried to gun me down out by Sandstone Lake last night. They set a trap for me. Their plan backfired. When you're finished putting Lancelot away, tell the doc Bolton is at Sagebrush Mine on the back side of Sandstone Lake and needs help. When we left him he was bleedin'."

Adam Carter looked at Wayne Thayer for a moment, pulled the kill list out of his pocket and said, "I'd like for you to hold onto this for me until I need it back, in case something happens. I know you aren't much help outside of Texas, but this is a list of men who are supposed to die today. I'm going to try and stop it."

"Is there anything I can do to help?"

"Just hold onto that list. Anything you do might give you away. I want you to remain above suspicion."

"You sure that's all I can do?"

"On second thought, I'd better have that list. I want it with me when the meeting starts. If anything should happen to me, you get the list back and send it to the U.S. Marshal's Office at Van Buren."

"I can surely do that, but don't you go getting killed."

"I'll try not to, but like I said, should anything happen."

Chapter 23

The meeting wasn't until ten that morning so Carter got things ready. If he could take charge of the meeting right off, he might be able to prevent unnecessary bloodshed. He knew the plans that Rosecrans had designed, but they were of no use to him now. What he had to do was make sure the men sent to kill the ranchers were notified in no uncertain terms about the death of Rosecrans. Whether or not Bolton had died as a result of his wounds, he didn't know.

In his hotel room, he cleaned up knowing full well if he laid down for a few minutes he would probably miss the meeting altogether. He was so tired, but he couldn't rest. Someone rapped on his door.

Stepping over to the door he said, "Who is it?"

"It's Duke Robinson, sir."

Opening the door he stepped back and holstered his pistol. "Come on in here, son. I want to speak with you."

Duke stepped into the room and Carter closed the door behind them. Duke was carrying his saddlebags, and Carter knew what was in them. "You getting ready to sign the deeds of certain properties back to their rightful owners?"

"For what good it will do, yes sir. All but Sagebrush Mine and Sandstone Lake, those are mine legal."

"You and Ian Durant," Carter said.

"Yes, sir."

"I see you're wearing two guns."

"Yes sir, one was my brother's."

"Every rancher for over a hundred miles will be at the Stockman's meeting this morning. I need you to back me up with that hardware. Stay far to the back of the room and don't let anyone get behind you, and don't pull those guns unless it becomes necessary."

"Sir?"

"Look, Duke, several men are supposed to die at that meeting and Bennett's one of them. I've got to stop it and I need your help. No one will suspect you of being my backup. Savvy?"

"I better not have this saddlebag with me then."

"No, get the papers you need out of it and leave the rest here. No one will bother them. I need your hands empty if it comes to a showdown."

Duke started going through the papers to separate the ones he needed. "Sir, I may be young and all or maybe I'm just not experienced in such things, but I don't see how we can have that meeting without a showdown."

Carter sat down on his bed and oiled his guns. When he was finished he tossed the small can of oil to Duke. "Here, make sure those things are in good working order because we surely will be called on to get them out."

Duke wasted no time getting is guns out and oiling them. He checked the action on both and dropped them back into their respective holsters. "What should I watch for?"

"My guess is there will be guns for hire in that room, hired to do one thing, kill the ranchers on this list." He showed the list to Duke.

"That's out and out murder!"

"That's right, and we've got to stop it. I've got to try and get Fowler to back me up as well."

"That might create more trouble. He wants me behind bars."

"I don't think so, Duke. He's known where you were for a few weeks. If he wanted you, he would have already arrested you and put you back in jail. He's been looking awful hard for somebody these last few weeks, hardly a soul in town has seen him. That man is on a mission and he's not worried about you."

Duke took a deep breath and relaxed. "You mean he's not charging me with murder?"

"He's been looking elsewhere, ever since the day you got shot. Refresh my memory, because I wasn't here yet, but wasn't that just a day or two after the two men were killed?"

"It was just twenty-four hours or so."

"Exactly, and he's been on someone else's trail ever since. If I were you, I'd relax about going back to jail. I don't believe you killed anybody and neither does Fowler.

"What we've got to do this morning may take an army, but all we've got is you, me, and maybe Fowler. That's a tall order. And Duke, I want you to keep a special eye on Kid Bradley if he's anywhere in the room."

"I don't know who that is."

"I'll point him out to you. I think he is supposed to eliminate me."

Duke cringed at the word eliminate. "What if they have someone assigned to eliminate me?"

"You'll be in the back corner of the room where no one can get the drop on you. You'll be watching the entire proceedings from there until I give the all clear."

A moment before Duke felt free, he was no longer a wanted man, now suddenly he felt like a duck in a shooting gallery. "Why don't we tell Mr. Bennett and his boys, Jack and Vance? They're downstairs."

"I don't want them primed for a gunfight. Any shooting will be done by us."

"But they would be good help."

"They could get us all killed if they pull iron in the middle of that meeting. Look, young man, whatever happens in there this morning, it's you, me, and Fowler. We can't trust anyone else."

"Man, when does a kid ever get to grow up?"

"What's that?"

"When does a kid ever get to grow up? All my life it seems as if someone is trying to kill me for some reason or another. Today seems like one of those days."

"I heard you once rode with Nathaniel Bowlin the Swamp Fox. Let me explain something, Duke. Things aren't going to change any time soon. Too many men from the war have become drifters, selling their guns for hire. We've got to deal with some of them today. We have to win. To do so we have to plan. No one knows who you are, at least not many. That's why I need you backing my play. You're my surprise, and you showed up at just the right time to defuse the entire situation.

"Now, I don't know if anyone has told you yet, but Duke, you are grown up. Get over it. You can't relive your childhood. Now, are you with me or not?"

Duke was stunned, but he managed, "I'm with you."

"All right, let's go see Fowler. I want him there with us."

The jailhouse was locked up tighter than a drum. No one was going to get in without a key, and no one knew where Fowler was.

169

"All right, Duke. Looks like it's you and me. Are you ready?"

"I'm as ready as I'll ever be."

The two walked down to the Devine Watering Hole and went in. A few men sat around, but in fifteen minutes the place was full of ranchers and men who wore guns. Duke stayed in the front corner where he could keep an eye on things, especially every man who walked in, but he was having second thoughts. He was worried about the last time he paid a visit to the place. He had promised he'd never set foot in another saloon for a drink. Well, this was business.

When Kid Bradley walked in, Duke recognized him immediately. Carter didn't even have to point him out. His swagger and youth gave him away. He walked right over to the table where Duke was sitting with his back to the wall and took a seat in front of him.

Rosecrans, Bolton, and Sanderson were missing, otherwise everyone was present, but some men were getting uneasy. Carter stood up on a chair and began the proceedings. "Men, this is an unusual meeting this morning. I want to start by saying, the firm of Rosecrans, Bolton, and Sanderson has been dissolved. They're no longer in business. If you're waiting to be paid for work you've done for them, you won't get it."

Everyone looked about the room to no avail, not one of the three men was present. A big burly man in the back of the room stepped forward. "What do you mean dissolved? How can that be? They owe me three hundred dollars!"

"It's simple my friend. Rosecrans is dead, Bolton was left for dead, and Sanderson isn't going to proceed without said partners."

"When did this happen? I spoke with Rosecrans just yesterday morning," the big fellow said.

"It happened last night just before the storm hit. The two of them tried to shoot it out with me."

Silence fell over the room. For a moment no one knew what to say and Carter was willing to let the news sink in before he spoke again.

"If any of you men are on the payroll of the firm you might as well pull out. There won't be any more pay. All assets of the firm have been frozen until everything has been sorted out."

The big man floundered. "Why, that could take a year or more."

Carter looked around the room then back to the big fellow. "Two or three more than likely."

There was grumbling from a few men scattered around the room and then one by one several gunmen got up and left. The last man to walk out was the big burly fellow who had spoken out. Once he was out of the saloon, Carter reached in his left vest pocket and took out the list, then continued.

"I have a list of names of the men who were supposed to die at this meeting this morning." Carter looked directly at Kid Bradley as he spoke. "No one is in any danger of dying. Not now," he said.

Just as Kid Bradley started to move, Duke put the muzzle of his six gun on his back. "Have a seat, and don't try anything," Duke said.

The kid leaned back in his chair and didn't move. He didn't turn around to look. Duke whispered in his ear. "I sure hope you don't have to cough or sneeze. If you make any move at all, and it won't matter why, I'll fill you full of holes."

Just then everyone looked toward the door. Someone was coming down the boardwalk and everyone in the room was primed to pull iron. When the culprit came into view it was Marshal Fowler with a young man in front of him. He shoved the fellow through the door and Duke almost choked. It was Ian Durant.

"We were wondering where you were," Carter said.

"I was rounding up some varmints."

"Looks like you found one, who is he?"

"Tell'em your name, boy."

"Ian Durant."

"Speak up boy, I don't think they heard you."

"Ian Durant!"

"That's better. Now, you want to tell them or shall I?"

"I ain't telling nothing. I didn't do anything."

"You are under arrest for murder, that's something."

"I didn't do it."

"Attempted murder, counterfeiting, and bank robbery."

"I didn't do anything."

"Duke Robinson, the first time we met was right here in this saloon. You had a go-round with a couple of fellows. They died that evening outside of town, and Ian here is the shooter. With them dead there were two less bank robbers to split the money with."

Ian stood with his hands cuffed behind his back, his head hung low. He was helpless in a room full of guns and the town marshal at his back. "I didn't do anything."

"I caught him out at the Sagebrush Mine near the back entrance in one of the cavern chambers. He was hoarding counterfeit money as if he didn't have enough from the bank robbery last year." Fowler tossed three heavy money bags onto the nearest table. "That's the money from the bank. I also found this rifle on him." Fowler pitched the rifle to Carter who looked it over.

"There's a back entrance?"

"Yes, but you have to know where to find it."

Carter looked at the rifle, then at Fowler. "I don't get it, what's this rifle got to do with anything?"

"Open the chamber and slip a round in it."

"All I have is a .45 pistol round, you know that."

"Exactly, now slip one in it."

Carter opened the ejection chamber and took a round from his gun belt. He slipped it in and closed the chamber.

"It's a perfect fit. He can shoot anybody he wants and you think you're looking for a pistol. He shot Duke with it."

"You shot me? Duke was beside himself and forgot about holding his gun on Kid Bradley. "You shot me?"

Marshal Fowler put his hand up. "Now hold on, Duke. He's unarmed and he's in my custody. I want you to keep your gun on Bradley because he was one of the bank robbers, and he's going to jail, too."

Duke looked at Kid Bradley for a long moment then brought his attention back to Ian. "You can jail him, but first he's going to sign these water right back to their respective owners. I've already signed off on them."

"I can't sign anything with my hands behind my back."

Fowler looked around the room at the ranchers. "Don't worry, I'll un-cuff you long enough to do that much, but don't get any ideas."

Kid Bradley was getting very fidgety and nervous. Duke, being so close to him noticed the change in his behavior. It happened the moment Fowler implicated him.

Fowler spoke again. "There's just one more thing to be settled. There was a map stolen from the bank safe that night, a detailed map that showed the proposed right-of-way for the railroad coming through Peace Valley. Jim, can you tell us where you put it?"

"No, I didn't have anything to do with it." The man who ran the land office looked around the room at the men he faced and found no reprieve. Jim Koch jumped straight through the front window of the saloon then scrambled down the boardwalk disappearing in a flash.

Fowler chuckled. "I'll round him up later, but you might as well know he was their ring leader. He planned the entire robbery. He only wanted the map, but if he got a little money in the process, well no one would know, isn't that right, Ian."

"That's right," he almost whispered.

"Louder."

"That's right."

It was all Kid Bradley could stand. He jumped to one side turning on his heel and dove out the other window before Duke realized what was happening. The owner of Sandstone Lake jumped over to the window just as a bullet spit the wood beside his face. He ducked back into the room and hit the floor. No one else had moved.

Fowler smiled. "It's all right, Duke, he isn't going anywhere. He's not going anywhere at all."

"But, he's getting away."

"He might run, but he's not getting away. He's nowhere to hide."

The room was quiet for a moment and then men began to talk. In a few minutes, the room was loud and full of noise. Harvey opened the bar, serving drinks on the house.

Duke holstered his pistol. Last time he was here it got him in real trouble. So far on this day, he was cleared of all wrong doing.

He walked up to Carter and handed over the deeds so Ian could sign off on them. Every remaining man in the Divine Water hole stood by to witness the event. Each one of the ranchers thanked Duke for putting them on their toes. As Ian finished signing the last one for Ferguson, Fowler picked him up from his chair and led him out the door then down to the jail.

Duke was watching from the front porch as someone stepped up behind him. Brooke took his arm. "Are we going to be okay, Duke?"

Realizing he was no longer a wanted man and the fact he was still alive, it was all Duke could do to keep from tearing up. "Are you sure you want someone like me? I seem to find trouble at every turn."

"Oh, Duke, I don't want anybody else," she said, searching his eyes.

Carter stepped up beside them. "Duke, I've got to go out to Sagebrush Mine and pick up at least one body, maybe two. That's your property, isn't it?"

"Yes, sir, that much belongs to me."

Good, we'll leave within the hour. Carter walked toward the jail. He still had a few things to clear up with Fowler. Eve came running across the street to greet him.

"Oh Adam, that was horrible. We heard gunfire, and we couldn't even check to see if you were okay."

"Well, now you know, I'm fine. So is everyone else. Kid Bradley and Jim Koch are on the loose, they were in on the bank robbery. Otherwise everything is fine."

"What happens now?"

"Well, I have to go pick up Rosecran's body and Charlie Bolton. Not sure what I'm getting into there, but Duke is going with me, it's his property."

"You be careful."

"You don't have to worry about that. I'll be watching my back, my front and both sides. I don't want anything to happen now. Not when everything is beginning to work out fine."

Chapter 24

When the two men reached the Sagebrush Mine vultures were circling in the sky above. Rosecrans's body lay where it was left, but there was no sign of Bolton. Somehow the man had managed to get onto his horse and ride away. The tracks led off toward the breaks to the west. Carter studied the tracks.

"I don't know if that makes my job easier or harder," he said.

"Might be both. Easier now, hard later."

"For a kid, you sure do have a way of putting things."

"It's my father's blood. I picked up a few things from him."

"Let's get Rosecrans's body back to town and see if we can't end this day on a good note."

As the work-filled days forced their way through spring roundup into summer, there was no sign of Bolton, Jim Koch, or Kid Bradley. It seemed as if all three men had literally vanished. The chill wore off the springtime grass with each passing day. The house up on Sandstone Lake began to take shape and Circle R cattle began to appear on the range. While Duke worked to build his home Brooke managed to find her way to his side quite regular. They worked together to erect a common dwelling, with plans of marriage when the home was finished.

Word came that the bank in Dodge City was robbed, and the description of the unidentified men fit that of

Bolton, Koch, and Bradley. There was no mistake so Marshal Fowler wired the law in Dodge to offer the names of the three suspects. A coach was robbed two weeks later and one of the passengers identified Black Bart the poet. No longer was there any question that Black Bart and Charlie Bolton were one and the same. There were two unidentified men with him. A one thousand dollar bounty was placed on the head of each man, Wanted, Dead or Alive.

By the end of summer whenever Brooke rode through Peace Valley, Duke Robinson was at her side. Notwithstanding the fact that a small number of reports concerning the three men made it to Duke's ears, the very lack of sufficient information caused his worry to mature.

"Duke, you promised we'd go explore the old mine sometime. Why don't we go today, we've got the time."

Duke was hesitant, thinking the last time he was there they picked up Rosecrans's body. It was an eerie place.

"I can't seem to go in that place but what I wish I was out. The way the walls surround you, the darkness deep within, it scares the daylights right out of me. If any one of those support beams ever fell or gave way while we were in there, we might never find a way out."

"We'd be together, Duke, and that's all I ask for."

They halted their horses for a moment overlooking Sandstone Lake. He looked into her eyes as their horses drank from the edge of the sprawling lake. "There's something to what you say, but I sure wouldn't want us confined in there the rest of our life. At least out here we can see other folks on occasion."

"But you have been there more than once, and I've never seen it. Vance says it is deeper than it looks. He said there are real interesting rock formations deep in the back, hollowed out rooms where you could camp out if you wanted."

"He sure has told you plenty."

"Oh Duke, I just want to see it, we don't have to go deep into it, can't we?"

Duke pulled his horse back from the water and turned in the direction of Sagebrush Mine. "All right, we'll go for a ride, but I don't want to explore the cave today. We'll just take a look at it."

They rode around Sandstone Lake and headed toward the breaks off to the west. The wide panoramic view of the land they would call home sprawled out before them as they rode.

On the other side of the lake sat the old man with the alligator boots. Duke watched as Brooke looked that way several times, but made no mention of the man.

"You told me once about the old hostler who was killed. Can you describe him for me?"

"He was a fairly big man, about six foot four, and he always wore dark green alligator boots. They're in the window at Scranton Lane's store. Nobody has ever been able to fit them, though many have tried."

"What about his clothes, his face, what did he look like?"

"He was a man with a very stern jaw. His eyes were piercing if he got riled, otherwise they were soft as a puppy dogs. He always wore tan pants and vest, and his shirt was usually some off red color." Brooke stopped her horse and looked at Duke. "Why is all that so important?"

Duke looked across the lake at the man she had just described and said, "No reason, I was just curious."

They rode in silence after that, each lost in their own thoughts. The only sound was saddle leather creaking and their horses' hoofs making contact with the soft ground. Then, almost without warning they were at the entrance to the mine.

Brooke slipped down from her horse and ran into the mine before Duke could stop her.

"All right, have it your own way," he said as he dismounted. He tied both horses to the hitch post near the entrance and ducked inside. All was dark.

"Brooke, where are you?" He was greeted by silence. "This isn't funny you know."

His eyes were slowly adjusting to the cave and he could sense someone's presence, but he couldn't see anything, not yet.

Duke was disgusted with himself...wishing he'd not allowed Brooke to talk him into bringing her here. He looked around at the walls, careful not to look back at the entrance and the bright light coming in. The walls seemed to close in around him like an evil giant and suddenly he wanted out, but he wasn't leaving without Brooke.

Brooke reached out and touched Duke from behind and he almost jumped out of his skin.

"Got ya," she said.

Duke was irritated. She wanted to play and this was no place for it.

"Duke, look!" she said as she pointed to a large boot print on the cave floor.

Thunder cracked outside and it started to rain. Duke turned to look and said, "We might as well make ourselves comfortable. I'll bring the horses in."

The animals were good and wet by the time he got them in, bringing Brooke's horse first. It was going to rain for a few hours, maybe all night. If it did that, what would he tell old man Bennett? He just wasn't going to buy any explanation Duke could think of.

There were some dry sticks in one corner and Brooke stacked them neatly to get a fire going. Once it was burning and Duke had the saddles off the horses they sat down and warmed their hands over the fire. Outside the storm raged.

"See, if we hadn't come here we'd be caught outside in all that rain." Suddenly she froze, her eyes locked onto something and the firelight reflected every ounce of fear in them.

He knew without turning to look what she saw, and for one crazy instant he thought about drawing his weapon as he turned, but it would have left her in the line of fire, and that wasn't something he could do.

"Well now, isn't this just peachy. Two lovebirds just looking for a place to light."

Duke's shoulders hunched as if he'd been struck. He didn't recognize the man's voice. Slowly he stood and turned.

"Really now, this is most favorable."

When Duke's eyes met those of the outlaw he knew the situation couldn't be any worse. All the neatness that had been associated with the man was gone. Black Bart was deshelved and no amount of sanity remained.

"Oh, this is just perfect, I get the plates so I can keep printing money, I get to kill you, and I get the girl."

"Where are the other two?"

"You mean Kid Bradley and Jim Koch? I killed them three days ago. They are back in the mine resting in eternal peace. They sure ain't going to need that money, real or counterfeit."

Duke was now facing the outlaw and shifted his position slightly. He was under the gun and didn't like being so close to Brooke in such a circumstance. He shifted his weight one more time and in that moment he knew Bart was going to draw.

Ready or not, he dove away from Brooke and palmed both revolvers. Something flashed in his eyes and pounded his ears at the same time, but he was firing both pistols, first one then the other until they were empty.

A look of shock overtook the outlaw's face. He tried to speak, but nothing came out. He pitched forward on the mine shaft floor and died. The look of shock was still etched in his eyes.

Thunder sounded outside only it was not near as loud as the guns that had just gone off inside the mine. Duke holstered his brother's gun and began reloading his own.

He turned from the man walked to the cave entrance and looked outside at the rain coming down. Then right where she belonged, Brook took him by the arm and stood looking out the cave entrance with him. They gazed out into a world all their own, whatever that meant. Whatever they could make of it, all of this was to be theirs.

As the two stood arm in arm, the old man in the green alligator boots rode up and stopped his horse in front of them. "I was beginning to wonder if I'd done the right thing, but you'll do."

Brooke apparently didn't hear or see a thing, only Duke.

"Those boots down at Scranton Lane's store, they'll fit you now. And take care of that girl."

"What is it Duke, what do you see?"

"Oh, nothing."

The man turned his horse and began to whistle Peace in the Valley. He faded out of sight while Duke watched. It wasn't every day a young man got to meet his own Guardian Angel!

Author Bio

The Author was born in St. Louis Missouri, August 1958. He is the middle son of three boys. After serving two honorable terms in the United States Marine Corps he got out and attended the University of Oregon so he could learn to write. His stint as a student was cut short by the untimely death of his daughter Kimberly Marie.

Realizing the professors could not teach him what he wanted to know he struck out on his own to become the self-taught author we know today.

Other books by John T. include:

OL' SLANTFACE
CAPTAIN GRIMES UNRECONSTRUCTED
BLOOD ONCE SPILLED
SHOWDOWN AT SCATTER CREEK
THE TREASURE DEL DIABLO
CATFISH JOHN

Signed copies are available at johntwayne.com

Artist Bio

Jim Clements is an oil painter who considers himself blessed to be a working artist. "To me, painting represents ultimate freedom - so it's just natural that the wide open spaces, rich history and independent people of the American West translate so well to canvas. My desire is to honor the spirit of the West in each painting I do." Working in newspaper illustration and advertising over two decades kept his drawing skills honed, as well as in his free time continuously painting. "Observations of life, as well as painting from life, are critical to artistic advancement," he explains. He also gratefully acknowledges the advice, instruction, and encouragement of many of today's best known oil painters throughout the years, who have been such an integral part of his own professional growth.

In addition to his website and galleries, Jim's award-winning work can also be seen at various Art shows and Western festivals throughout the year. His work is collected internationally and has won numerous awards over the years. His paintings have been featured in various magazines and are in the permanent collection of The Coutts Memorial Art Museum in El Dorado, Kansas. He was also the solo artist at a show in the Woolaroc Museum in Bartlesville, Oklahoma. After New York television producer Robert Rose saw them, several of his American Indian paintings were featured on an episode of Raw Travel, which is aired world-wide.

Jim's home and studio are located on the prairie in the Flint Hills region of south central Kansas.

Anyone who does research into American history may have to swallow a bitter pill from time to time. When you realize that every state in the Union was a sovereign entity prior to the Civil War and the Federal Government could not tell the states what to do, it sheds new light on the subject of States Rights. When the war ended, every Yankee Doodle Dandy in the north and every Swinging Dixie in the south handed their sovereignty over to the Federal Government. That means every state in the Union lost, not just the south. The men listed below died that we might remain free. Had the northern soldiers known in the end they would also hand their sovereignty over to the Federal Government, I don't believe a single man would have picked up a rifle.

Hamilton Parks, Jr.	14th TN Cavalry Co. K
John Luther Parks	12th TN Cavalry Co. K
Andrew Stewart Parks	12th TN Infantry Co. K
Pinkney Bell	10th TN Cavalry Co. K
Kinchen B. Foster	10th AR Infantry Co. D
Robert Steele Irvin	7th TN Cavalry Co. D
Moses E. Yarbrough	In memoriam

9 781645 705291